Reading Nabokov's Framed Landscape

Maya Minao Medlock

佛教大学研究叢書

英宝社

Reading Nabokov's Framed Landscape

Maya Minao Medlock

EIHŌSHA

TABLE OF CONTENTS

Acknowledgements v

Introduction 1

Chapter I: Nabokov's Passion for Landscape 7

Chapter II: Nabokov through Windowpanes 44

Chapter III: Mapping out Fyodor's Berlin 78

Chapter IV: Following Fyodor's Footsteps 107

Conclusion 149

WORKS CITED AND CONSULTED 153

Acknowledgements

This book grew out of my doctoral thesis completed at Kyoto University a long time ago. It would have been buried forever without a grant generously given by Bukkyo University. I owe them an enormous amount for their giving consent to the publication of this volume. I would also like to thank Mr. Shimomura Koichi from Eihosha for his support.

I would like to express my deep gratitude to the members of the Kyoto Reading Circle, discussions with whom have always been inspiring and instructive to me, and especially to Professor Wakashima Tadashi, without whose invaluable instruction and constant encouragement I could not have finished the present work. I also would like to extend my thanks to Timothy Medlock, my husband, who patiently corrected my English and made numerous suggestions for more suitable English expressions.

Reading Nabokov's Framed Landscape

Maya Minao Medlock

Introduction

Vladimir Nabokov in his pseudo-review of his autobiography *Speak, Memory* points out that the author's method is "to explore the remotest regions of his past life for what may be termed thematic trails or currents."[1] He encourages the reader to "enjoy finding for himself the convolution, the stepping stones, the various smiling disguises of this or that thematic line running through the book" (*SM* 239-40). After introducing some of those themes, he continues: "All thematic lines mentioned are gradually brought together, are seen to interweave or converge, in a subtle but natural form of contact which is as much a function of art, as it is a discoverable process in the evolution of a personal destiny" (*SM* 240). Toward the end of the book, according to the pseudo-reviewer, the theme of mimicry "comes to a punctual rendezvous with the 'riddle' theme," and "[t]o the same point of convergence other thematic lines arrive in haste, as if consciously yearning for the blissful anastomosis provided jointly by art and fate" (*SM* 240-41). Incidentally, Nabokov, under the mask of his own reviewer, here represents the "method" of intertwined themes through the metaphor of trains, one of the recurrent motifs in the autobiography itself, and thus firmly (but secretly) interlocks this review with the memoir. Moreover, by (re)using this rather rare word "anastomosis," which is actually what Nabokov uses in Chapter 7 of this book, he cleverly succeeds in linking this part to the phrase "a parallel rail line all at once committing suicide by anastomosis" (*SM* 113) (so the two phrases meet together by anastomosis).

As Alexandrov states, Nabokov's art (not only *Speak, Memory*) is char-

---

[1] *Speak, Memory: An autobiography Revisited.* 1967. London: Penguin, 1999, 239. Henceforth as *SM*. Citations from Nabokov's works will be keyed into the text with abbreviations of the title followed by the page number. Nabokov first published his autobiography under the title of *Conclusive Evidence* (1951), and then another version in Russian as *Drugie berega* (1954), and finally *Speak, Memory*. I have used the 1999 Penguin edition, which includes "Appendix: "Chapter Sixteen" or "Conclusive Evidence."

acterized by "the kind of intricate 'braiding' of strands of motifs;" "one connects with another, which branches into others, and so on."[2] The most pleasurable, ideal and productive way of reading Nabokov's works, therefore, seems to be to find motifs and themes, and to discover the "garden paths and park walks and forest trails" (*SM* 241) that connect those, drawing a labyrinthine map of his world.

The present dissertation, being faithful to this method, will pick up first a certain basic motif and then discover the paths leading to yet another motif or theme, repeating this pattern until the end, where those themes and motifs all join together, by the "blissful anastomosis." Our main interest will be *The Gift*,[3] which, because of its highly autobiographical components,[4] could be approached through finding and combining themes, following Nabokov's advice.

In the first chapter we will begin with the theme of a "finger-drawn picture," or the motif of a "white pencil." In *Speak, Memory*, Nabokov recalls and reproduces an invisible landscape of his favorite path leading to his summer house, which was drawn by the 5-year-old Nabokov's forefinger—his primitive yet most imaginative pencil. We will acknowledge this transparent landscape (or map) as one of his first artistic works and even as the original image of some works by Nabokov characters in future, clarifying how a colorless writing implement could produce the most colorful

---

[2] Alexandrov, Vladimir E. *Nabokov's Otherworld*. Princeton: Princeton UP, 1999, 49.

[3] Nabokov, Vladimir. *The Gift*, Translated by Michael Scammell with the collaboration of the author, 1963. New York: Vintage, 1991. For quotations from the English version, I have used this edition; the Russian text used throughout is the Symposium edition. In this thesis, since *The Gift* (*Дар*) is the work we mainly deal with, page references are to the translation first, and the original second, without the title.

[4] Dolinin mentions Alexandrov's discovery of "a complex network of interrelated motifs (childhood illnesses, footstep, house-room-door-key, etc.)", which reminds us of the system found in *Speak, Memory*. (Dolinin, Alexander. "The Gift," in *The Garland Companion to Vladimir Nabokov*, ed. Vladimir E. Alexandrov [New York: Garland, 1995], 139.)

Introduction

and imaginative pictures. Also we will explore the relationship between the visual art and the verbal art in Nabokov's work. We will focus on his distinguished mastery of verbal translation from a visual work of art, which is termed "ekphrasis."

Chapter II will be a close scrutiny into "the window motif," which proves to be somewhat inseparable from the theme of painting and landscaping examined in the previous chapter. First we will gain a general notion how windows work in several works; next we will focalize our concern on the train window motif in particular; finally we will discuss the window motifs found in *The Gift*.

Chapter III is an attempt to produce a map of Berlin that is described by Fyodor Godunov-Cherdyntsev, the protagonist and the possible narrator of this novel. In the first section we will clarify the topographical problem in this novel, focusing on the scattered squares and public gardens, which are marked by various benches—a motif that will be under examination in the second section. We will prove how the bench scenes reveal the complicated theme of "consciousness" both of the narrator and of the protagonist, and how benches serve as a guide, a sign, to show us something unusual is happening in the narrative. In addition to this, we will examine the relationship between the theme of "double" and the bench motif observed especially in Nabokov's early works, which would support our argument.

In the last chapter we will explore how the act of "walking" plays a dominant role in *The Gift*, introducing the motif of entrance / exit. By walking with Fyodor and finding limitless paths, we will imagine an invisible, never realized map of his Berlin. One of the entrances leads us to another motif of "the letter," of which study will occupy the first part of the chapter. Here we will find out that Fyodor's last letter in the novel works as a hidden entrance of this novel itself; also this letter clarifies how the Berlin night itself could be a possible heroine of this novel.

−3−

Reading Nabokov's Framed Landscape

Vladimir Vladimirovich Nabokov led a uniquely peregrine life. Until 1977 when he finally settled himself in a hereafter—the land of his life-long interest—he had always been with his suitcase like most of his protagonists. He was born in 1899 in St. Petersburg. After finishing his study in Cambridge University, he moved to Berlin, where he met and married Véra Slonim and spent two prolific decades as a Russian writer "Sirin" (Nabokov's Russian pen name signifying the legendary bird with a woman's face and breast). After a short stay in France, he fled to the United States in 1940, where he underwent a marvellous but "painful"[5] transformation from the Russian Sirin to an American author Nabokov. After another two decades of living as an American citizen, he returned to Europe, where he spent the rest of his life—again nearly two decades. Throughout his life, beginning with poetry, he produced more than sixty short stories, some plays, works of translation and more. He wrote nine Russian novels and eight in English, a total of seventeen works among which *The Gift*, our main concern in the present thesis, finds itself in the very center position.

The Gift (*Dar*), Vladimir Nabokov's last, longest and finest Russian novel, was first serialized in the émigré journal *Sovremennye Zapiski* in 1937-8. It was published in 1952, and its English translation was completed in 1963 by Dmitri Nabokov and Michael Scammell with revision by the author. Here a brief explanation about the two "version" of this novel should be made. The text we use cannot exactly be called a "translation": this is, as the translator Scammell himself calls in his recent interview published in *Nabokov Online Journal*, "a version", "a performance" of "rare power and fidelity" on the author's part, for his first translation "has been overseen by the author," who "practically rewrote some passages".[6]

---

[5] Nabokov, Vladimir. *Strong Opinions*. New York: Vintage, 1990, 54. Henceforth as *SO*.

[6] Nabokov in his Foreword to *The Gift* says he "carefully revised the translation of all five chapters".

−4−

Introduction

Therefore, we are treating not "a mere translation."[7] The English version *The Gift*, therefore, is as respectable and proper a work of art as the Russian original (version) of it, thus deserving equal appreciation. This is indeed a multilayered, complex, and highly self-referential work. Also, Scammell points to the extraordinary subtleness and refinement of the "love interest", that is, the "central relationship between Fyodor and Zina", as well as the "extremely cerebral" nature of the novel as potentially explaining "the relative lack of success" of *The Gift* among a non-Russian audience.[8] Still, this is not a work that spurns a non-Russian reader's ignorance of Russian literary and political history let alone the first Russian emigration. The book is brimming over with moments of bliss, magic, and tenderness and limitless imagination; the plot is not very active, progressing rather quietly and gently, and this quiet tenderness, outstanding tonality of this book compared to other Nabokov works, makes the novel approachable. Nabokov hid in this seemingly alien, unfriendly book his most generous, glamorous, smiling lines full of rich images and ideas to be discovered by a lucky reader.

Nabokov's last Russian novel paved in Berlin new paths leading to a homeland that is situated beyond both space and time. The novel focuses on the life of Fyodor Godunov-Cherdyntsev, a young Russian émigré living in Berlin. The story spans three years (from April 1, 1926 to June 29, 1929) of the protagonist's life, which is marked with the publication of his collection of poems, literary evenings, change of lodgings, the romance with Zina Mertz, and the publication of his *Life of Chernyshevski* (a biog-

---

[7] Scammell, in response to the interviewer Leving, expressed his "dislike" against Leving's "use of the adjective 'mere' in front of 'translation'. "All translations," he continues, "even bad ones, require a huge amount of knowledge and a huge amount of labor to complete, and though translators have come to be regarded as the donkeys of the literary profession , their work deserves better than that (and how can a translation by Nabokov be 'mere'?)" ("Translation is a Bastard Form". *NOJ*, 2007.)

[8] See "Translation is a Bastard Form". *NOJ*, 2007.

−5−

raphy that occupies Chapter 4). Through his collection of poems depicting his childhood, through his attempts to write a biography of his heroic father and his published biography of Nikolay Chernyshevski, and a novel that is beginning to take shape toward the end of the book, we can witness Fyodor's maturation as a writer. His émigré life, for all his alienation and repulsion, is depicted with full of beauty, goodness, generosity and wonder; it is illustrated as a life brimming with gifts. At the same time the novel seems to show Fyodor's gratitude to everyone and everything to whom he owes those gifts. His grateful feeling, however, is expressed not immediately but with delay, by the narrator's varied voices. And the relationship between character Fyodor and the narrator (the author of *The Gift*) is one of the most difficult problems in this novel.

The work could be considered an example of various genres: a love story, a Künstlerroman, a portrait of a young artist, a dedication to Russian Literature, etc. It has still more aspects, which we will find now, following Fyodor's peregrination in Berlin, stepping from one motif to another.

Chapter I
Nabokov's Passion for Landscape

1. A Picture drawn with a Finger

Reading any work of Vladimir Nabokov compels some readers to grab a pen to work out at least two things: a map of the main site and illustrations (with colored pencils, if possible). The more one gets to know the world of Nabokov's art, the keener one feels the importance and use of these minor creations on the part of the reader. It is true that making a list of characters and chronology is also useful. In the present dissertation we will limit our concern to a reading of Nabokov based on visual art.

An episode recounted in *Speak, Memory*, Nabokov's autobiography, leads to the notion that Nabokov's inclination for maps / landscape seems to have germinated already in his early childhood. Nabokov as a five-year-old child in a villa his family rented on the Adriatic already shows his art of recreating the past:

> … mooning in my cot after lunch, I used to turn over on my stomach and, carefully, lovingly, hopelessly, in an artistically detailed fashion difficult to reconcile with the ridiculously small number of seasons that had gone to form the inexplicably nostalgic image of "home" (that I had not seen since September 1903), I would draw with my forefinger on my pillow the carriage road sweeping up to our Vyra house, the stone steps on the right, the carved back of a bench on the left, the alley of oaklings begging beyond the bushes of honeysuckle, and a newly shed horseshoe, a collector's item …,

shining in the reddish dust of the drive. (*SM* 61)

The five-year-old boy tries to map out the paths on his white pillow with his finger, reproducing a retreated landscape in his memory. Moreover, that he should do so based on a memory formed by the time he was aged only three testifies to his extraordinary power of retainment.

This five-year-old Nabokov, with such a creative finger as his writing / picturing implement, prefigures the mature artist Vladimir Nabokov. This invisible map (landscape) drawn by his forefinger—his primitive yet most imaginative pencil—could be recognized as one of his first artistic works and even as the original image of some works by Nabokov characters in future.

Also noticeable is the fact that it is the 60-year-old Nabokov who recollects and describes the 5-year-old, who, in his turn, recollects his past: "The recollection of that recollection is sixty years older than the latter, but far less unusual" (*SM* 61). More interesting is that Nabokov as a mature artist freshly delineates again this "still transparent" (to borrow his own expression found in *The Gift*) picture drawn originally by the child Nabokov. To put it in another way, Nabokov is visually reproducing, this time by using a pencil, an invisible picture drawn on the pillow. What happens here is a series of translations: first the little Nabokov translates a memorized scenery into an invisible picture on his white pillow, then the adult Nabokov translates it into words, and finally the reader translates it in his / her mind into an visual image, thus reconstructing the original landscape that is full of color, sound and life. The forefinger of the boy, therefore, seems to be a primitive figure of writing materials—a pencil (Nabokov's favorite was a pencil, not a pen)[1] or a paintbrush—and we can say that it is highly creative, imaginative and, paradoxically, colorful.

---

[1] Nabokov allows the reader a glimpse of the way he writes this memoir: "I, who write my stuff only in very sharp pencil, keep bouquets of B3's in vaselets around me" (*SM* 146).

Chapter I Nabokov's Passion for Landscape

This passage is full of details which are closely linked to the themes this dissertation deals with, and before comparing with other Nabokov works, we need to note still a couple of further features by which this passage is marked.

When closely observing this memory-based picture (and almost a map), we will notice one striking detail that seems quite different in nature from other details.[2] Representation of the carriage road, the stone steps, the back of the bench and the alley of oaklings is relatively normal: these are the details anyone could perceive anytime, for they are practically unchangeable, without being subject to time. The concluding detail, however, is quite different from the others in terms of tone, or tinge: "and a newly shed horseshoe, a collector's item ..., shining in the reddish dust of the drive." As the word "newly" suggests, the horseshoe has just appeared there, that is, it cannot be part of an unchangeable, timeless view but exists in one particular moment. Most impressive is its shine, which becomes the focal spot to which our eyes are inevitably attracted. It is amazingly ingenious for a boy of five to delineate by finger the shine of that special horseshoe thrown just *now* in the field of his memory. We could even say that these two words (precisely, "two details," for we are actually talking about a picture, not a phrase)—"newly" and "shining"—are what make this passage (this picture) extraordinary. This is a picture that seems to be based on the young Nabokov's general memory of the place, and not on the memory of one specific day. However, in this repeatedly perceived, thus time-free landscape (not being bound to any specific time) the boy lovingly embeds something quite particular and momentary. It is, however, not so extraordinary and unique as far as Nabokov works are concerned:

---

[2] In *Drugie berega*, the Russian version of his memoir, has more interesting details not found in the English version, such as "a puddle with a catkin and a dead beetle". See *Vladimir Nabokov. Drugie berega (s parallel'noi publikatsiei angliiskoi versii)*. Moscow: Zakharov, 2004, 95.

–9–

Nabokov frequently uses this very device—concealing something momentary and specific in a landscape that is disguised as a repeated, general scene—in many works, of course in the form of language, not picture. This pattern enables the momentary object to take on a special tenacity, endowing it with eternal life. What is extraordinary in the present passage is that the old Nabokov again follows the child's finger to restore its original glimmer and freshness.

Usually he smuggles in these passages marked by a mixed time by using the auxiliary verb "would." We will examine the matter later in chapter III of this thesis, together with the theme of "bench," which, incidentally, appears in this very passage too as "the carved back of the bench." [3]

The last point to clarify about this passage is the meaning of what the 5-year-old Nabokov is doing here. The image worth examining may be the finger following the beloved path "carefully, lovingly, hopelessly": "Carefully," for he must imagine and produce (reproduce) an invisible path, as a blind man who believes in the presence of the road ahead of him and tries not to lose it; "lovingly" he follows the path as if he were caressing a girl he loves; this promenade, however, is only an imagined one, a recollection, one that he can never realize, therefore "hopeless." Now we have the impression that his finger, feeling the surface of the path, identifies itself with his feet. The young Nabokov's feet could almost feel the earth of this beloved avenue through his finger. It might be said that this is a kind of synesthetic moment: he could feel the sensation derived through his finger as that of his feet.

Also the reader keenly feels with all their senses the tender, almost amorous touch with which his finger delineates the admired path; we can feel even its undulation (though it is not mentioned), smooth curve of the back of the bench, and maybe the scent of honeysuckle. This affectionate,

---

[3] Quite possibly this may be the bench depicted in *The Gift* where Fyodor in his imagination revisits the paths towards his summer villa.

Chapter I Nabokov's Passion for Landscape

dreamy, amorous touch reveals another hidden motif: place associated (or identified) with a beloved woman. Nabokov's depiction of the streets or a city itself is sometimes, somehow, linked with a woman, and this theme we will discuss in the last chapter, where we will examine "letters theme", especially in the context of *The Gift*.

One of the main themes of *The Gift* is "walking," and Fyodor finds a pleasure and importance in walking barefooted. So the sensation of the earth felt through the bare foot is a dominant feeling throughout the novel: this way of generating topography in the world of his work by making a character feel the street with his own feet (or by the tires, in the case of, for instance, *Lolita*) is closely connected to what the 5-year-old Nabokov did—to feel the path and to reproduce the map with his finger. This passage, therefore, contains some essential themes of Nabokov works, and it can be seen as a rich source of details which connect *Speak, Memory* to many other works.

Now we will start to examine those details by focusing first on his novel *Invitation to a Beheading*. We can find a good many reflections of the passage especially in the sequence of the "Tamara Gardens" view. As we have seen, Nabokov's finger seems to be the original of all the writing instruments. The invisible picture (it also serves as a map for him to go back home) drawn by the finger is astonishingly detailed and unique. The image of the 5-year-old boy Nabokov following by his finger the remembered paths reminds us of a certain passage in his novel. The protagonist Cincinnatus, sentenced to death for the crime of "gnostical turpitude," stays in prison throughout the whole story. [4] He still keeps believing in the existence of his "dream world" (*IB* 93), which consists of "the originals of those gardens where we [Cincinnatus and Marthe, his wife] used to roam" (*IB*

---

[4] Nabokov, Vladimir. *Invitation to a Beheading*. Trans. Dmitri Nabokov in collaboration with the author. 1959. New York: Vintage, 1989, 72. Henceforth as *IB*.

−11−

94) outside the prison fortress, which is only "a shabby, vulgar copy." The "gardens" mentioned here mean a huge public park called "Tamara Gardens," on which his memory quite often casts its light.

The gardens first appear in the protagonist's imagined walk outside the prison tower. He, however, does not enter the gardens, only recalling several discursive details lovingly and nostalgically. Therefore the gardens are still inaccessible even in his imagination.

The Tamara Gardens next appear in Chapter 2, when the narrator details Cincinnatus's past, especially about how he met Marthe. The narration, however, seems to glide into Cincinnatus's own recollection. The passage describing the gardens is devoid of the word "he," which would indicate Cincinnatus, and the voice changes from the neutral to a rather impassioned one, talking about such personal details as Marthe's "white stockings," "velvet slippers," "cool breast" and "rosy kiss." The passage ends in the following manner: "If only one could see from here—at least the treetops, at least the distant range of hills…" (*IB* 28). Here, the narrator is speaking in the voice of Cincinnatus's, who is "here" in this prison and not "there" ("here," "there" are repeated in the text, showing the remoteness of the garden from the prison). What is important is that the narrator dares not to describe the gardens beyond Cincinnatus's knowledge and memory. Such a way of narration produces the impression that the Tamara Gardens are almost unattainably distant and hidden both from the protagonist and from the narrator.

Most curiously, the description of the gardens develops according to the same pattern we have found in the description of that pillow picture. It begins with casual, common and timeless details: "the willows weep into three brooks, and the brooks, in three cascades, each with its own rainbow, tumble into the lake, where a swan floats arm in arm with its reflection" (*IB* 27-28). We note that the narrator begins to depict from the highest point and gradually goes downward, delineating the natural flow (movement) and direction of, first the willows, second the brooks and then

−12−

Chapter I Nabokov's Passion for Landscape

the cascades, and finally the lake, so that the reader could visually recreate
the landscape from the top, following the natural flux.

The narration leaves the water site and starts to picture the lower place:

The level lawns, the rhododendrons, the oak groves, the merry gardeners in their green jackboots playing hide-and-seek the whole day
through; some grotto, some idyllic bench, on which three jokers had
left three neat little heaps (it's a trick—they are imitations made of
brown-painted tin), some baby deer, bouncing into the avenue and
before your very eyes turning into trembling mottles of sunlight—
that is what those gardens were like! (*IB* 28)

Here we have the impression that the focus of the description is coming
nearer and nearer towards us (coming forward), allowing us to recognize
small, particular details. These details, compared with the willows, the
brooks, and the cascades that form an almost unchangeable, timeless and
impersonal background, appear quite specific; it sounds as if it were based
on Cincinnatus's own personal memory of one specific day. As Connolly
points out, "the three little heaps" are one of "disquieting elements" that
spoil the "alluring vista,"[5] and the appearance of the gardeners almost
turns this otherwise romantic scene into a farcical one, therefore, unlike
the case of that perfectly idyllic, ordered pillow picture, these focal points
are there to disclose something not right hiding in the Tamara Gardens.

The last detail, however, restores beauty and wonder to the scenery. As
already mentioned above, the passage, as that pillow drawing, begins with a
general detail and ends with a specific one, focusing on one remarkable object: "a baby deer turning into trembling mottles of sunlight," which corresponds to that shining horseshoe in the finger picture on the pillow. It
must be noted that the mixture of the general and the specific is one of the
factors by which Nabokov's style is marked.

---

[5] Connolly, Julian. *Nabokov's* Invitation to a Beheading: *A Critical Companion*. Evanston: Northwestern UP, 1997, 19-20.

−13−

The reader thus manages to visualize a part of the huge gardens. This evocation by the narrator is followed by a description inside the prison room, where Cincinnatus tries to see the remote gardens from out of the window, which is itself "way, way up high" (*IB* 28) and as remote and unattainable as the gardens.

In the next chapter, he finally gets a distant view of the Tamara Gardens from the terrace of the top of a tower. However, they are still too vague and distant to assure they are really there, so they cannot be recognized as "the original." What Cincinnatus really gazes at is just "the glimmer and haze of" the gardens (*IB* 43).

"Reality" of this view is possibly first harmed by the following expression: "Far below one could see the almost vertical vineyards, and the creamy road that wound down to the dry river bed; a tiny person in red was crossing the convex bridge; the speck running in front of him was most likely a dog" (*IB* 42). The description here has a striking resemblance to the view from "Chestnut Court" (also "Crest," or "Castle") depicted by Humbert Humbert in *Lolita*.[6] Alter renders a precise observation on the entire passage including the following paragraph, explaining how "we are taken into the magic of its presence by being made to see it as a painting." [7] According to Dolinin the part quoted above is an allusion to *Hunters in the Snow* by Brueghel.[8] Whatever the source is, this Brueghelian expression inevitably inclines us to regard the view as somewhat artificial, as a reproduction of some work of art, not the original. While Cincinnatus seems to be able to see the surrounding scenery together with small details,

---

[6] Nabokov, Vladimir. *The Annotated Lolita*, ed. with preface, introduction, and notes by Alfred Appel, Jr., 1970; rev, ed.: New York: Vintage, 1991, 212-13. Henceforth as *Lo*. For a discussion of these two scenes, see the next section in the present chapter.

[7] Alter, Robert. "*Invitation to a Beheading*: Nabokov and the Art of Politics." In *Nabokov's* Invitation to a Beheading: *A Critical Companion*. 47-65, 55.

[8] Dolinin, Alexander. "Notes" in *Vladimir Nabokov. Sobranie sochinenii russkogo perioda v 5 Tomakh*, T4, St. Peterburg: Symposium, 2000, 615.

Chapter I Nabokov's Passion for Landscape

the lawyer who leans his elbow on the stone parapet near him only "peered pensively into space, his left patent-leather shoe placed upon his right" (*IB* 43).[9] He is just peering into "space," quite possibly being blind to what Cincinnatus clearly sees. Or, we could conclude that the view is really invisible, that is, does not exist to the eyes of anyone but Cincinnatus.

A similar thing happens in, for example, "Cloud, Castle, Lake" (1937), Nabokov's favorite story of his own and a story directly connected to *Invitation*. The protagonist Vasiliy Ivanovich (though the name is not quite reliable, as the narrator admits being unsure about his hero's name), during a train trip from Berlin that he was not really inclined to make, sees a beautiful view of a blue lake reflecting a large cloud and a black castle. His fellow German travelers, however, seem not to notice, or at least not to be attracted to, the scenery, as in the case of *Invitation*: the leader of the group, for example, "sat on a stump, his behind to the lake."[10] The only person who sees the lake is Vasiliy Ivanovich and it is almost invisible to the rest. The distant view of "the lake with its cloud and its castle" (*Stories* 435), just as the distant view of the Tamara Gardens from the fortress, seems so ephemeral and even artificial that its very existence seems doubtful.

Vasiliy Ivanovich dreams of staying permanently in the room with a window through which one can get a perfect view of the lake, but they do not allow him to do this, forcing him to come back with them to Berlin. Incidentally, Vasiliy Ivanovich, claiming a right to stay where he likes, cries: "Oh, but this is nothing less than an invitation to a beheading" (*Stories* 436). After this he is dragged back to the train and tortured by them al-

---

[9] The picture of the lawyer here somewhat reminds us of Nabokov's representation of a pencil sketch drawn by Pushkin for *Eugene Onegin*, which shows "the author and the hero leaning upon the Neva parapet" (*EO II* 176). Nabokov's treatment to illustrations for *EO*, including the sketch in question is subject to analysis in the next section.

[10] Nabokov, Vladimir. "Cloud, Castle, Lake" in *The Stories of Vladimir Nabokov*. New York: Vintage, 1995, 430-37, 435. All further citations from this text will be noted by a parenthetical reference containing the abbreviation *Stories* and the page number.

−15−

most to death. The end of this story, therefore, "points to the novel *Invitation to a Beheading.*"[11] The two worlds have much in common, and actually quite resemble each other. As Shawen notices "the doomed fragility of Vasili [sic] Ivanovich's vision",[12] this view has the same illusory quality as the Tamara Gardens. They are both that Baudelairean "Là, tout n'est qu'ordre et beauté, / Luxe, calme et volupté"—somewhere far away and inaccessible.[13] We will later study this short story more closely, but now let us return to the theme of Tamara Gardens.

It can be concluded that here Cincinnatus sees the detailed view including the glimmer of the gardens not with his eyes but with his imagination and memory. This special eyesight reinforced with imagination and memory is shared by many other Nabokov characters.

The third appearance of the gardens is in the form of a replica. This scene especially deserves close scrutiny, for it shows two central motifs with which we are concerned: the window motif and what might be termed the motif of "digital delineation." For the moment we will limit our discussion to the latter.

Cincinnatus, walking along the corridors of the fortress, finds "a deep window" which proves to be only "the semblance of a window," a "showcase," displaying "in its false depth . . . a view of the Tamara Gardens" (*IB* 76). The narrator continues to describe it in detail:

> Everything was reproduced fairly accurately as far as grouping and perspective was concerned, and, were it not for the drab colors, the stirless treetops and the torpid lighting, one could slit one's eyes and imagine oneself gazing through an embrasure, from this very prison, at those very gardens. The indulgent gaze recognized those avenues,

---

[11] Shrayer, Maxim. *The World of Nabokov's Stories.* Austin: U of Texas P., 1999, 161.

[12] Shawen, Edgar McD. "Motion and Stasis: Nabokov's 'Cloud, Castle, Lake'", *Studies in Short Fiction*, 27: 3 (1990: Summer), 379-383, 382.

[13] The link between this couplet from *L'invitation au voyage* and the repetitious evocation of Tamara Gardens beginning with "*There*" is generally agreed on by critics.

Chapter I Nabokov's Passion for Landscape

that curly verdancy of groves, the portico at the right, the detached
poplars, and, in the middle of the unconvincing blue of the lake, the
pale blob that was probably a swan. Afar, in a stylized mist, the hills
humped their round backs, and above them, in that kind of stale-
blue firmament under which Thespians live and die, cumulus clouds
stood still. (*IB* 76-7)

Especially the last part of the depiction above, incidentally, with its "blue
of the lake" and cumulus clouds that "stood still," echoes that too perfect
view of the "blue lake" with "its cloud and its castle" (as if they were the
belonging, equipment, of the lake) in the story "Cloud, Castle, Lake" (*Stories*, 435). Displayed beside the replica of the Tamara Gardens, the view in
the short story reveals its artificial nature more clearly, and looks more like
a replica, with a "motionless" and inseparable trio (lake, a cloud and a castle).

The narrator continues: "And all of this was somehow not fresh, anti-
quated, covered with dust, and the glass through which Cincinnatus was
looking bore smudges, from some of which a child's hand could be reconstructed" (*IB* 77). The smudge here could be attributed to the hand of
Emmie, an enigmatic child who Cincinnatus believes has a key for him to
escape out of prison, and is now beside him. He even asks her: "Won't
you please take me out there?", as if Cincinnatus believed that she is the
author of, or at least the person who is responsible for the replica, as he
earlier in the story attributed a set of pictures forming "a coherent narrative, a promise" of his escape to Emmie (*IB* 61). The sentence concluding
this scene shows an image already familiar to us: "He was sitting next to
Emmie on the stone projection and both of them were peering into the artificial remoteness beyond the glass; enigmatically, she kept following
winding paths with her finger, and her hair smelled of vanilla" (*IB* 77).
Here, Emmie's finger duplicates that creative weaving of the 5-year-old
Nabokov's finger. In *Speak, Memory*, the old Nabokov is carefully watching
the child Nabokov delineating and reconstructing the past landscape, fol-

-17-

lowing the transparent paths and reproducing them in the form of language, thus making them visible. In doing so, Nabokov can revisit an irretrievable place in the past. This child, therefore, serves as a medium through which the old man launch himself into an imaginary promenade in his aspired past. What Cincinnatus expects from the little girl here may be more or less the same: identifying Emmie's weaving finger with his own feet, Cincinnatus is trying to realize a dreamed promenade through the garden paths. Although Emmie is not the childhood figure of the hero, unlike the case of *Speak, Memory*, it is likely that she plays, to a certain degree, the part of the hero's double; more precisely, she seems to represent his childhood. There figures are marked commonly by blond hair; Emmie sitting on "a sill-like projection of stone" and peering into the artificial remoteness beyond the glass" recalls the figure of the child Cincinnatus who "was sitting with [his] feet up on the low window sill and looking down" on the school garden and then "stepped straight from the window sill onto the elastic air" (*IB* 96-97). The two scenes certainly form companion pictures. The child Cincinnatus is also looking down the garden, which is not the idyllic Tamara Gardens but the school garden, which he does not want to descend into, and he half succeeds in "slip[ping] out of the senseless life" (*IB* 96) by stepping from the window sill. However, in both cases he fails to go out of the glass and so escape from the present life.

Also, he is repeatedly described as a child or even a baby, and even feminized by M'sieur Pierre, first allegedly his "neighbor" but really his executioner, who calls him "my fair damsel" (*IB* 78) and with whom he goes to "an informal supper" at the suburban house, which appears to be represented covertly as a wedding of Cincinnatus and Pierre. Pierre and Cincinnatus are shown, though not directly, respectively as the groom and the bride. The atmosphere of a wedding in this whole event is especially endorsed by the following remark made by Cincinnatus's brother-in-law: "Afraid, aren' t you? Here, have a drink on the brink" (*IB* 184). We cannot see any allusion to a wedding here in the English version, inferring, rather, the mention of an execution. The Russian original, however, reads as follows: "*Boyazno, podi? Vot hlebni vintza do bentza*" ("Afraid, probably? Drink wine before the wedding"). Also, "a recent best man" cries "Bitter, bitter, sweeten it with a kiss" (*IB* 185), which corresponds to the Russian "*Gor'ko!* (Bitter!)," a common, repeated cry in a Russian wedding.[14] These facts invite us sometimes to see Cincinnatus as a girl, even allowing us to see some family resemblance between them.

Emmie's relationship to Cincinnatus, therefore, seems to be almost the same as the child Nabokov's to the old author: the child in both cases is in a way the grown-up's alter ego (even the 5-year-old Nabokov as represented in a work of art is not quite the same person as the adult Nabokov, the child's biographer, and they are two entities as different as Cincinnatus and Emmie). Emmie, however, proves not to be as helpful as the child Nabokov.

Comparing the description of the view from the fortress with that of its replica, we do not find a major difference between them in terms of "reality." The "real" view from the tower is therefore as artificial as the replica and far from the original. As Cincinnatus believes: "*There, there* are the originals of those gardens" (*IB* 95), the original must be "there," hopelessly far away and almost unattainable. It exists only in his memory or in his imagination, thus irrecoverable.

This idea is highlighted in the fourth appearance of the Tamara Gardens, which prove to be where "the suburban house of the deputy city manager" (*IB* 180), the site of the banquet briefly mentioned above, is situated. The following passage shows the moment when Cincinnatus realizes he is in the very gardens:

Standing by the balustrade, Cincinnatus peered vaguely into the

---

[14] *Priglashenie na Kazn'. Vladimir Nabokov. Sobranie sochinenii russkogo perioda v 5 Tomakh*, T4. St. Peterburg: Symposium, 2000, 44-187, 161.

−19−

darkness, and just then, as if by request, the darkness paled enticing-
ly, as the moon, now clear and high, glided out from behind the
black fleece of cloudlets, vanished the shrubs, and let its light trill in
the ponds. Suddenly, with an abrupt start of the soul, Cincinnatus
realized that he was in the very thick of the Tamara Gardens which
he remembered so well and which had seemed so inaccessible to
him." (*IB* 186-87)

First of all we should find it strange that Cincinnatus does not realize
the fact that he is in the longed-for gardens until the moonlight replaces
the darkness. This scene is represented as if it were a sudden shift of scenes
in the theatre: only the protagonist does not follow this abrupt change.
We have the impression that with quite a dramatic rise of the moon the
hero is suddenly, unexpectedly transported to the next scene, and there appear now props and scenery in the space which only a black void, darkness,
had occupied.

Cincinnatus experiences another "sudden" change of the scenes earlier
in this episode. The narrator explains how "vague and insignificant" the
"nocturnal promenade" from the fortress to the suburban house is and how
quickly it "flashed by" (*IB* 181). Moreover he is made to wear a cowl,
which could interrupt his view, so the whole itinerary, covered with "the
integers of night" (*IB* 181), is almost unknown to Cincinnatus. Also,
though the walk to the gardens should take an extremely long time, the actual one "flashed by," which creates the impression that he (and also we)
reaches the destination in an instant. At the end of this nocturnal promenade, when he reaches "the end of a narrow and gloomy lane," there "suddenly appeared a theatrically lighted carriage porch with whitewashed columns, friezes on the pediment, and potted laurels . . . ." (*IB* 181). In both
cases, the abrupt shift of the scenes occurs with darkness replaced by a
sudden burst of light, taking on the atmosphere of a theatrical effect.[15] .
This atmosphere of theatricality enhances the artificiality of the gardens itself.

Chapter I Nabokov's Passion for Landscape

After realizing he is in the center of the gardens, Cincinnatus:

... easily removed the murky film of night from the familiar lawns and also erased from them the superfluous lunar dusting, so as to make them exactly as they were in his memory. As he restored the painting smudged by the soot of night, he saw groves, paths, brooks taking shape where they used to be .... (*IB* 186)

What he is doing here is to correct and revise the present, real scenery, based on his memory—the original. Most importantly, the narrator likens the view to a painting, of which "original" may be found not in the "real" place, here, but in the gallery of Cincinnatus's memory, in the past. Incidentally, the process by which Cincinnatus reproduces "the painting" recalls that transparent drawing on the pillow. The original landscape of both pictures are now gone, but the pictures are made as closely as possible to their original, by the power of language. What Nabokov did in his autobiography was to translate the picture into language. In doing so, he renders the scenery visible for himself and for us, and even animates it (because words can show what a drawing cannot show), and makes it reach the closest point to the original. Nabokov, with the original landscape in his past, can follow the paths and relive the place by delineating the transparent drawing with his pen, more correctly, with his pencil, as Nabokov in his memoir shows us himself writing in the narrative present: "I who write my stuff only in very sharp pencil, keep bouquets of B3's" (*SM* 146).

Cincinnatus's case is a little more complex. If we read only the passage above we are inclined to conclude "the originals" of the gardens are in Cincinnatus's memory. In reality, they do not exist even in his memory because he has been living in this world of "copy" since he was born. This

---

[15] The theatrical image in *IB* has been widely discussed. Nabokov stresses the theatricality to show how they see the "execution as spectacle" in this world; it also "underscores the sham, derivative nature of the beings who inhabit this space" (Connolly, Julian. "Introduction" in *Nabokov's* Invitation to a Beheading: *A Critical Companion.* Evanston: Northwestern UP, 1997, 9-10).

Reading Nabokov's Framed Landscape

"memory," therefore, may also be only a copy, a fake. The originals could be found in his imaginative, creative power, that is, it is Cincinnatus himself who will imagine and create the original—through language. "Cincinnatus is striving to use language," says Johnson, "to break through the strictures of this world and describe an ideal world."[16] His "ideal world," as we already saw, are where "the originals" are found. As Johnson suggests, he has to imagine and describe with language what the originals are like, for his ideal world to exist. Maybe the original is an illusion, just as the cases of Tatiana's letter that is supposed to be "originally" written in French in *Eugene Onegin*, Charlotte Haze's letter to Humbert Humbert in *Lolita*, or Sebastian's letter in *The Real Life of Sebastian Knight*, as Wood points out while discussing the act of translation from a really absent "original" into a text of different language.[17] However, a real writer, an author of a work of art, which Cincinnatus wants to be, can believe in and imagine, thus "recreate," even the nonexistent original.

By now we have seen how the images in the first pillow drawing are reflected in the novel *Invitation to a Beheading*, especially in the descriptions of the Tamara Gardens. Now we will clarify how the motif of finger following remembered paths and then drawing an invisible landscape is closely connected to the theme of "a white pencil."

In Chapter 5 of *Speak, Memory*, Nabokov shows us his colored pencils "in action." After describing the working of the green, the blue, the brown, the red and the purple (his favorite), he introduces the special pencil:

The white one alone, that lanky albino among pencils, kept its original length, or at least did so until I discovered that, far from being a

---

[16] Johnson, D. Barton. *Worlds in Regression: Some Novels of Vladimir Nabokov*, Ann Arbor: Ardis, 1985, 42. A revised version in *A Critical Companion* has the word "walls" instead of "strictures" (*Critical Companion* 134)

[17] Wood, Michael. *The Magician's Doubt: Nabokov and the Risks of Fiction*. Princeton: Princeton UP, 1995, 145.

Chapter I Nabokov's Passion for Landscape

fraud leaving no mark on the page, it was the ideal implement since I could imagine whatever I wished while I scrawled. (*SM* 79-80) When he draws something with the white pencil on a white page, he produces an invisible picture, which naturally recalls the transparent landscape drawn on the pillow with the forefinger. The white pencil is a magic instrument with which he can freely create anything. Most importantly, this pencil never impairs his imagination: it "kept its original length" until he realizes its magic, but once it begins working, it should keep faithful to "the original" imagination, for it never taints the original image. The motif of pencil itself, incidentally, pervades Nabokov works: in *Invitation*, for instance, the length of Cincinnatus's pencil is always in question: in Chapter 8 Cincinnatus's pencil "had lost more than a third of its length" (*IB* 89); in Chapter 11 it "had lost its slender length and was well chewed" (*IB* 120); finally in chapter nineteen, after he crosses out the word "death," he stops writing completely, with a "stunted pencil" in his fingers (*IB* 206). Interestingly enough, we cannot know what happens to this pencil in the end: it becomes suddenly invisible. He says (though the narrator admits he "did not say all this"): "My papers you will destroy, the rubbish you will sweep out, the moth will fly away at night through broken window, so that nothing of me will remain within these four walls" (*IB* 211), but the whereabouts of his pencil remain unsaid, as if it had totally disappeared. The possible answer to this question is that Cincinnatus keeps his pencil with him forever, as the only key to escape out of this world. The pencil, the instrument used to create his ideal world, is so important a thing for him that it finally seems to dissolve into a part of his existence.[18] .

We should also mention how subtly and in what a timely manner Nabokov slips this episode of colored pencils into that particular narrative.

---

[18] For further discussion on the theme of pencil in this novel, see Barabtarlo's "The Informing of the Soul" in his *Aerial View: Essays on Nabokov's Art and Metaphysics* (New York: P. Lang, 1993).

−23−

Reading Nabokov's Framed Landscape

The chapter in which this episode is told is originally called "Mademoiselle O"—a portrait of Nabokov's French governess. The pencil episode is inserted in the passage illustrating the approaching Mademoiselle on the snowy street and the anticipating children in the house. Though the story of pencils with the white one as its hero seemingly interrupts the main plot, it is in fact subtly planned and is far from a digression.

The present passage evokes Mademoiselle on the sleigh, on the night street covered with snow, so it must be dominated by the white of the snow. Curiously, the inside of the house where the child Nabokov and his brother and Miss Robinson (the present governess) are waiting for her is painted white in places: here is "a footman's white glove," "the gleaming white moldings of furniture," and the "white piano" (*SM* 100). Also they are all in a drawing room "in a snow-muffled," therefore white, house. The dominant color of the scene is apparently white: the white pencil in the author's mind must be in full action. Another important keyword is "imagination." The long passage describing Mademoiselle's arrival from Switzerland is not based on Nabokov's actual memory but on his imagination:

> When she alighted at the little Siverski station, from which she still had to travel half-a-dozen miles by sleigh to Vyra, I was not there to greet her; but I do so now as I try to imagine what she saw and felt at that last stage of her fabulous and ill-timed journey. (*SM* 77)

Nabokov can "visualize" her clearly "by proxy"—"his ghostly envoy," who "offers her an arm that she cannot see" (*SM* 77). Following her through the eye of this invisible man, he continues to describe her travel in detail, using his unreserved imagination. So the basic idea here is shared by the work of a white pencil, with which "I could imagine whatever I wished." As he can imagine and create what he never saw with the magic white pencil, he can create through his imagination the governess's travel, the scene he never witnessed, himself being as transparent as a picture drawn with the white pencil. This is therefore the right place for the episode of

-24-

Chapter I Nabokov's Passion for Landscape

the colored pencil (especially the white one) to be recounted.[19]

Nabokov continues: "Alas, these pencils, too, have been distributed among the characters in my books to keep fictitious children busy" (*SM* 80). Among those is Fyodor in *The Gift*. Sitting on a bench—a highly privileged device in Nabokov world[20] —Fyodor and Zina, his love, talk about "crayon pencil":

> "But then the sharpened ones. ... Do you remember the white one? Always the longest—not like the red and blue ones—because it didn't do much work, do you remember?"
>
> "But how much it wanted to please! The drama of the albino. *L'inutile beauté.* Anyhow, later I [Fyodor] let it have its fill. Precisely because it drew invisible and one could imagine lots of things. In general there await us unlimited possibilities. ..." (192; 372-73)

Fyodor's idea about the white pencil is exactly the same as Nabokov's manifested one in *Speak, Memory*. So Fyodor is bequeathed the pencil together with the idea itself: those pencils are one of the "gifts" from Nabokov to the protagonist.

There talk develops into the theme of again "imagination:"

> "Yes, I [Zina] also think we can't end here. I can't imagine that we could cease to exist. In any case I wouldn't like to turn into anything."
>
> "Into diffused light? What do you think of that? Not too good, I'd say. I am convinced that extraordinary surprises await us. It's a pity one can't imagine what one can't compare to anything. Genius is an African who dreams up snow. ..." (192-93; 373)

Fyodor's remark here shows a pivotal concept in this novel: to imagine

---

[19] The colored pencils belong to "the rainbow theme," to borrow the author's own words. Though this episode is only treated as a part of various other color images, the theme itself is thoroughly discussed by Johnson in terms of synesthesia in his *Worlds in Regression*.

[20] For the bench theme see chapter 3 of the present thesis.

what cannot compare to anything. The biggest thing among those must be death, or the world after death, which we will discuss in the section that deals with the "window" theme. Fyodor here mentions the snow as an example: this is also a recurrent motif (not only in *The Gift* but in other Nabokov works including *Speak, Memory*) that is sometimes accompanied by the theme of imagination, as we have already seen in the passage picturing Mademoiselle's journey. Also *The Gift* has an impressive scene where the snow falling on the ground of the past Petersburg drifts into the present city of Berlin (80; 263); the same type of snow scene can be found in the short story "The Visit to the Museum" (1939), where the narrator visits a museum in a town in the south of France, but finds himself at the end of the visit on a street in Russia, covered with snow.

The white pencil—a developed form of the child Nabokov's finger—is an ideal instrument for Nabokov: the best way of depicting the invisible, the inscrutable, may be to do so by means of an invisible color. Being a color but at the same time almost colorless, white could be tinged with every imaginable color possible. This is a free color, full of possibility and therefore, paradoxically, the most colorful color of all (the opposite is of course black, the most restricted, that is, imprisoned, color, which dominates the biography of Nikolay Chernyshevski written by Fyodor).

These set motifs—the invisible painting, color-free writing materials—are related to another recurrent motif of "transparency." While depicting Mademoiselle reading to the child Nabokov and his brother, his pen follows the child's wandering attention to the colored windowpanes: "the most constant source of enchantment during those readings," he remembers, comes from "the harlequin pattern of colored panes inset in a whitewashed framework on either side of the veranda" (*SM* 84).[21] He continues:

---

[21] See Naumann, Marina Turkevich. *Blue Evenings in Berlin: Nabokov's Short Stories of the 1920s.* New York: New York UP, 1978, 196-97. Naumann briefly notes variations of the "window-pane images" in this brilliant work on Nabokov's short stories.

Chapter I Nabokov's Passion for Landscape

The garden when viewed through these magic glasses grew strangely still and aloof. If one looked through blue glass, the sand turned
to cinders while inky trees swam in a tropical sky. The yellow created an amber world infused with an extra strong brew of sunshine.
The red made the foliage drip ruby dark upon a pink footpath. The
green soaked greenery in a greener green. And when, after such
richness, one turned to a small square of normal, savorless glass,
with its lone mosquito or lame daddy longlegs, it was like taking a
draught of water when one is not thirsty, and one saw a matter-of-
fact white bench under familiar trees. But of all the windows this is
the pane through which in later years parched nostalgia longed to
peer. (*SM* 84)

In this passage we can catch the same intonation that is used in the description of those colored pencils. Among other colored panes, Nabokov
privileges the colorless, transparent one, as he chose the white one among
the colored pencils, and what is in common is the fact that the delight of
the colorlessness comes afterwards: he always starts to appreciate them
"later" (the same applies to Fyodor). Here the view through this "normal,
savorless glass" is written through the metaphor of a glass of water. The
mentally satiated child Nabokov did not notice the treat lurking in the
depth of this plane, transparent glass, while, once he is far away from
home, what he aspires for is quite naturally just a clear view, unimpaired by
any taste nor superfluous color: the pure-water like garden view that could
appease his thirst for the past, original scenery.

Colored glass can dramatically change and enrich the original landscape, which looked attractive only to the eyes of the child. To him, who
wishes to glimpse an unusual world (that is, "the otherworld") behind the
everyday, too familiar world, these colored magic films are quite handy and
useful. On the other hand, to the eyes of the grow-up Nabokov, who can
never see the view any more, this once "familiar," daily view ceases to be
"matter-of-fact" and familiar, and the view itself, without any make-up nor

−27−

help from colored glasses, is now endowed with an otherworldly nature and charm.

Nabokov's love for transparency and white pencil reveals his aspiring for "the original" and his wish to be faithful to his own imagination. A transparent, invisible picture drawn with a white pencil (or with his finger) on a white background must be the most colorful picture, and the closest form of what he imagines. Colored pencils have their limits, as Nabokov himself admits: "Their detailed spectrum advertised on the box but never completely represented by those inside" (*SM* 79), unable to represent exactly what he imagines. On the other hand, a colorless pencil could produce the most colorful picture, based on an unlimited, imaginative, and yet unnamed, color in the author's mind. Therefore the white pencil and his forefinger really contain every possible color existing (and also those not existing) in the natural world and in Nabokov's mind. The artist Nabokov sees these transparent pictures not with his "physical eye, that monstrous masterpiece of evolution," but with his "mind, even more monstrous achievement"[22] and translates them into his own language. This reproduction of an invisible picture in the form of words retains the original freshness, glimmer and exactitude. His writing pen may be a substitute for the white pencil; now the writer Nabokov can create anything he wishes neither with a white pen nor with a finger, but with a black pen, as the form of literature. And it is the reader who is expected to complete this chain of translation: "Nabokov, as a painter with words, expects the reader to translate verbal description into visual ones."[23] Our unreserved imagination could restore the original colors to the black and white page.

---

[22] Nabokov, Vladimir. *Lectures on Literature*, ed. by Fredson Bowers. New York: Harcourt Brace Jovanovich/Bruccoli Clark, 1980, 3. Henceforth as *LL*.

[23] De Bries, Gerard, D. Barton Johnson with an essay by Liana Ahenden. *Vladimir Nabokov and the Art of Painting*. Amsterdam: Amsterdam UP, 2006, 20.

Chapter I Nabokov's Passion for Landscape

2. Nabokov and Ekphrasis

What could be termed a twin picture of that invisible drawing on the pillow appears in Chapter 4 of *Speak, Memory*. Noticing a considerable number of descriptions concerning pictures, we are tempted to rename this chapter, originally called "My English Education," "My Passion for Drawing." In this section we will briefly study Nabokov's portrait as a painter-writer. Before examining the picture mentioned above, we should first clarify Nabokov's admiration for visual art, and how highly he was thinking of making illustrations during the process of reading a book.

According to Johnson and de Vrie, there are more than 150 references to painters in Nabokov's works.[24] His works also abound with references to fictional painters and paintings, and with numerous descriptions about sundry visual materials, such as posters, advertisements, postcards, picture books and so on. One of Nabokov's obsessions, therefore, is to delineate a visual work with his pencil and translate it in the form of language, which is the method traditionally called "ekphrasis."[25]

As the detailed maps and precise illustrations inserted in Nabokov's Lectures on Literature suggest, to produce sketches seems to be an indis-

---

[24] De Bries and Johnson. *Art of Painting*, 19.
[25] The term "ekphrasis," consisting of "ek" (out of, from) and "phrazein" (to tell, pronounce), originally meant "telling in full," (Heffernan, James A. W. *Museum of Words: Poetics of Ekphrasis from Homer to Ashbery*. Chicago: U of Chicago P, 1993, 191) or "a full of vivid description" (Wagner, Peter. Ed. *Icons—Text—Iconotexts: Essays on Ekphrasis and Intermediality*. Berlin: de Gruyter, 1666, 12). The term "has been variously defined and variously used and that the definition ultimately depends on the particular argument to be deployed" (*Icons* 13). In the present dissertation it is used to refer to "the verbal description of visual representation" (*Museum of Words* 3). The first attestation of "ekphrasis" in European literature is a detailed description of Hephaestus making a shield for Achilles in the eighteenth book of the Homeric *Iliad*. For an ample examination of the matter see Becker, Andrew Sprague. *The Shield of Achilles and the Poetics of Ekphrasis*. Lanham: Rowman & Littlefield, 1995.

– 29 –

Reading Nabokov's Framed Landscape

pensable factor that forms the art of reading a book. To put it in another way, a book that does not excites him to draw any sketches or maps cannot be said to be a proper work, or at least an ideal work, for Nabokov. His works themselves consist of those passages which inspire us to draw illustration from them, for he, being "born a painter,"[26] is "writing as a painter."[27] It is clear that the reader is also expected to produce some sketches from his words, as he himself did during his reading. This process can be regarded as one form of translation. The ideal reading of a work by Nabokov may be in a certain sense to translate his language into a visual image, hence the opposite of ekphrasis.

His interest in the relationship between a literary work and illustrations as a form of its translation can be clearly observed in his commentary on Pushkin's *Eugene Onegin*:[28] this gigantic commentary is full of references to (and complaints about) his predecessors' versions of the work, but his comments on what could be termed visual translations cannot be dismissed either. The best example is his commentary on Chapter 1, stanza XLVIII, where Onegin and Pushkin are in conversation on the Neva embankment. First Nabokov presents a letter in which Pushkin draws his own idea of a picture for *Onegin* and asks his brother to find "a skillful and prompt illustrator" for the first edition of Chapter 1 (*EO* II 176). Then Nabokov sets out to reproduce with his words "a good reproduction of that pencil sketch": Pushkin contemplating the river; Onegin in profile; a sailing boat; the Peter and Paul fortress. This "translation" from the poet's rough picture scribbled with a "rapid pencil" into detailed, expressive words

---

[26] Nabokov, Vladimir. *Strong Opinions*. 1973. New York: Vintage, 1990, 17. Henceforth as *SO*.

[27] *Art of Painting*, 16.

[28] *Eugene Onegin. A novel in Verse by Aleksandr Pushkin*. Trans. with commentary by Vladimir Nabokov, 2 vols., Bollingen Series 72. Paperback edition. Princeton: Princeton UP, 1990. All further citations from this text will be noted by a parenthetical reference containing the abbreviation *EO* I or II and the page number.

−30−

Chapter I Nabokov's Passion for Landscape

occupies half a page, in which Nabokov seems to stick to his favored "literal translation," that is, "rendering, as closely as the associative and syntacti-
cal capacities of the original" (*EO* I viii). His description is so detailed,
careful, and sensitive, that from it the reader could correctly reproduce in
the margin of the page Pushkin's pencil sketch again.

After rendering his faithful, model reproduction, Nabokov introduces a
version drawn by "the miserably bad artist, Aleksandr Notbek:"

> The boat has been deprived of its sail; some foliage and part of the
> wrought-iron railings of a park, the Letniy Sad, have been added
> along one margin; Onegin wears an ample fur carrick; he stands
> barely touching the parapet with the palm of his hand; his friend
> Pushkin now blandly faces the spectator with his arm crossed on his
> chest. (*EO* II 177)

As he is wont to compare his own (verbal) translation with other translators' versions and expose their blunders and misreading, he juxtaposes his
own precise interpretation and Notbek's quite arbitrary visual rendition:
he proves how Notbek cut such details as a sail, how he added such superfluous scene as the Letniy Sad (Summer Garden), and how he blindly mis-
read Onegin's "hourglass-shaped, long-skirted frock coat with two back-
waist buttons" as "an ample fur carrick," [29] and how he twisted Pushkin's
body, which should really "be seen from behind" (*EO* II 176), to face the
observer.

Most curious thing is that Nabokov quotes here "an amusing epigraph"
that Pushkin composed in reaction to this "little monstrosity" on the part
of Notbek:

> Here, after crossing Bridge Kokushkin,

---

[29] Nabokov, generously enough, explains to the reader in advance, in his note on "beaver
collar" (*EO* II 70-71), that an "ample-sleeved *shinel*" is a "glorified capote or, quite exactly, a furred carrick." Nabokov's concept about dresses is also always clear and detailed.

−31−

With bottom on the granite propped,
Stands Aleksandr Sergeich Pushkin;
Near M'sieur Onegin he has stopped.

Ignoring with a look superior
The fateful Power's citadel,
On it he turns a proud posterior:
My dear chap, poison not the well! (*EO* II 177-78)

Nabokov also reproduces Notbek's "even worse daub" for "Tatiana writing to Onegin," which represents "a portly female in a clinging night dress, with one fat breast completely bare," together with Pushkin's "some licentious lines" drawn from this picture. What Nabokov is trying to show here is a curious chain of translations: Pushkin (re)translates into a verse from a picture into which Notebek translated from Pushkin's verse and sketch. The final products (Pushkin's "epigram" and "licentious lines") prove to be only a grotesque parody of the original (Pushkin's lines in *Onegin* and his sketch). This endless chain of nightmarish translations reminds us of a similar phenomenon Nabokov tells in his essay "The Art of Translation."[30] Here we are shown how Nabokov translated ("reversing") into English K. Balmont's (whose own works Nabokov says disclose his inability to "write one single melodious line") Russian version of Edgar Allan Poe's "Bells"; he then imagines the sequence to that:

> Now, if somebody one day comes across my English version of that Russian version, he may foolishly retranslate it into Russian so that the Poe-less poem will go on being balmontized until, perhaps, the "Bells" become "Silence." (*LRL* 318)

Nabokov therefore proves that what could happen in a visual translation is essentially the same as what could happen in a verbal one.

---

[30] Nabokov, Vladimir. *Lectures on Russian Literature*. Ed. Fredson Bowers. New York: Harcourt, 1981, 315-21. Henceforth as *LRL*.

Chapter I Nabokov's Passion for Landscape

Nabokov concludes the note mentioned above with "the funniest picture" by Notbek depicting "an enormous female calmly sitting on a horse as on a bench, with both her legs dangling down one flank of her slender microcephalous white steed, near a formidable marble mausoleum" (*EO* II 178-79). When he describes even a picture of "lunatic," that is, a bad translation, he still remains as faithful and detailed as when reproducing the original, so that the reader can easily retranslate it into a picture, which completes the whole sequence of translations. His keen interest in the endless chain of translations could be detected in places, for example in his significant note on stanza XXXIX of Chapter 4, where he explains how Pushkin himself adopted "literalism" as a method of translation, which Nabokov defines as "absolute accuracy" and regards as the only acceptable way of translation. Concerning for the word "*belyanka*," which Pushkin accurately derived from the words "une blanche" used by André Chénier, Nabokov states that "the English translator should reincarnate here both Pushkin and Chénier." (*EO* II 465).

Nabokov also never fails to describe any little sketches on the margin made by Pushkin himself, regarding them as equally important materials with verbal sources. From his delightful hand we can imagine his excitement to know Pushkin was, as Nabokov himself was, particular about visual image and needed perfect illustration to his work. This quest for illustration is one of the themes in "Ultima Thule," Nabokov's short story, the narrator of which, unlike other Nabokov narrators, is a painter, and who is commissioned to make a series of illustrations for the epic poem "Ultima Thule" by its author, a "strange Swede or Dane—or Icelander" (*Stories* 510). They can only vaguely communicate each other with French, and in spite of the fact that the author is "unable to translate his imagery for me [the narrator]," the author nevertheless asks him this job. With "translation" and "illustration" as its leading themes, this story seems to be a thoroughly twisted parody of Pushkin's concept of illustration revealed in *Eugene Onegin*.

−33−

We must now return to the point of departure and take a look at the pictures in Chapter 4 of *Speak, Memory*. What we termed "a twin picture" of the drawing on the pillow is shown in the following, famous episode: [31]

> In an English fairy tale my mother had once read to me, a small boy stepped out of his bed into a picture and rode his hobbyhorse along a painted path between silent trees. While I knelt on my pillow in a mist of drowsiness and talc-powdered well-being, half sitting on my calves and rapidly going through my prayer, I imagined the motion of climbing into the picture above my bed and plunging into that enchanted beechwood—which I did visit in due time. (*SM* 68)

The picture in the tale and the real picture above the child's bed overlap each other in his imagination, and moreover, through the motifs of pillow and of path between the trees, the already two-folded picture could naturally be united with another picture, that is, the one the child Nabokov draws on his pillow. The overlap seems never to stop, for the scene above inevitably recalls still another scene, where the child Nabokov is kneeling on his pillow at the window of a sleeping car to see a marvelous nightscape of a light-scattered hillside (*SM* 20), which we will examine in the next chapter as a "train window motif." It can be said that the framed picture here is transformed into a framed window, through which the boy can step out. Therefore, though it might sound rather conventional, it is clear that in Nabokov's world a picture and a window are always ready to be merged, or interchangeable.

In Chapter 4 of the memoir Nabokov also introduces to us his drawing teachers, from whom the child learnt a tremendous joy of painting, wonder of colors, and each of whom had a great influence on Nabokov's later verbal art too. The first teacher shown is Mr Cummings, who had taught his mother too, and who "was a master of the sunset" (*SM* 72).[32] His translation into language from Cummings' drawing is so vivid and enchanting as

---

[31] Almost the same episode is related in his novel *Glory*.

Chapter I Nabokov's Passion for Landscape

to almost convey the blissful rush of the author's pen. His pen, as if it was tracing the lines drawn by Cummings, reproduces them with words. Even a rather dry, colorless process of learning is rendered attractively:

> Silently, sadly, he illustrated for me the marble laws of perspective: long, straight strokes of his elegantly held, incredibly sharp pencil caused the lines of the room he created out of nothing (abstract walls, receding ceiling and floor) to come together in one remote hypothetical point with tantalizing and sterile accuracy. (*SM* 72)

After he learnt "not only to draw cubes and cones but to shade properly with smooth, merging slants such parts of them as had to be made to turn away forever," Cummings, under the boy's "enchanted gaze," sets out to paint "his own wet little paradises, variations of one landscape: a summer evening with an orange sky, a pasture ending in the black fringe of a distant forest, and a luminous river, repeating the sky and winding away and away" (*SM* 72). Nabokov's enchanting description, which makes the reader visualize the wet, fresh watercolors and even makes these pictures look like real landscapes, really expresses the boy's enchantment. Nabokov's portrait of Cummings mixing paints on his palette, producing a honey-like color and then drawing, is particularly splendid, resembling both a portrait and a kind of landscape painting in which the painter himself is painting another landscape.

Dobuzhinski, a celebrated painter, also taught Nabokov and made him "depict from memory, in the greatest possible detail" objects he had seen thousands of times "without visualizing them properly" (*SM* 73). So, from Cummings he learnt colors, lines and structure, while from Dobuzhinski how to reconstruct images from memory, and what he learnt from both lessons is clearly reflected in his later literary composition.

In the same chapter, Nabokov's subject of translation from a picture

---

[32] Olga, in *Bend Sinister*, who is remembered drawing sunsets, seems to be his direct pupil (*Bend Sinister*. London: Penguin, 1974, 14).

– 35 –

Reading Nabokov's Framed Landscape

into language extends to children's picture books. Most curious is that by
being delineated with Nabokov's pen, originally stable, flat pictures and
characters come to look three-dimensional and become animated, so his
pen seems to give them life. He narrates now the adventures of his favorite Golliwogg and his friend-dolls that appear in "large, flat, glossy picture
books"[33] : "We see them in the dead of night stealing out of doors to sling
snowballs at one another until the chimes of a remote clock . . . send them
back to their toybox in the nursery" (*SM* 65). Is he describing this part intentionally to mix his real world with the fictional world, the real nursery
with the fictional one? After this, he mentions a picture he "really dis-
liked," in which "a rude jack-in-the-box shoots out, frightening my lovely
Sarah." He continues:

> Another time they went on a bicycle journey and were captured by
> cannibals; our unsuspecting travelers had been quenching their
> thirst at a palm-fringed pool when tom-toms sounded. Over the
> shoulder of my past I admire again the crucial picture: the Golli-
> wogg, still on his knees by the pool but no longer drinking; his hair
> stands on end and the normal black of his face has changed to a
> weird ashen hue. (*SM* 65)

The description itself is fresh, vivid and animated, conveying his admiration, but again a frightening image concludes the passage. He also recalls
"the motorcar book" with "the usual sequel—crutches and bandaged
heads," and concludes this picture book episode with the forlorn image of
"Midget," who, as an "aeronaut", "drifted into an abyss of frost and stars—
alone" (*SM* 66). We must notice that the descriptions of his favorite picture books always end with a cruel, violent scene, in spite of the fact that
we can at the same time sense his admiration for the picture and excitement. We see these dolls start to move freely and cheerfully in the text by

---

[33] According to Johnson, the book in question is *The Adventure of Two Dutch Dolls*. By
Florence K. Upton.

Chapter I Nabokov's Passion for Landscape

the magic of Nabokov's words, but at the same time his precise verbal description unexpectedly discloses a constant cruelty lurking beneath the pictures. This cruelty may not necessarily be indicated explicitly, but sometimes through his accurate translation into expressive language a hidden dimension to the picture clearly emerges.

One of the characters who follows Nabokov's destiny—a writer born to be a painter—is Fyodor, the protagonist (and possibly the narrator) of *The Gift*, who is, according to the narrator, destined for "really not literature but painting" (27; 214). Compared with such works as *Ada* and *Bend Sinister*, the number of references to pictures in this novel is not necessarily big, but still the narrator's translations from pictures into language look too delightful to be ignored, and it is essential for us to study the way visual art is treated and how pictures play a significant role in this novel. (Ekphrasis in *The Gift* includes a highly detailed description of an "illustrated cover" for the carton containing a toy: on the cover is painted a family, and the children there, says the narrator, "have now grown up and I often run across them in advertisements" [13; 200-201]. The theme of "development" or "growth" is observed here, which is one of the leading themes in this novel. Incidentally, "developing" advertisements recall a series of vivid circus posters—another fine example of ekphrasis—in "Spring in Fialta," each of which looks curiously different and conveys the atmosphere of gradually approaching circus to the town.)

The theme of visual art evolves around Romanov, a painter of Fyodor's age, whose "cold narrative art" and "a certain trace of the cartoonist's style" with its rich detail and playfulness somewhat reminds the reader of Fyodor's style, and he himself admits some affinity between the painter's art and his own, saying that he is "thrilled by Romanov's strange, beautiful, yet venomous art," and that he perceives in it "both a forestalling and a forewarning: having far outdistanced my own art, it simultaneously illuminated for it the dangers of the way" (59; 244). First, Fyodor willingly reproduces Romanov's celebrated early work "Four Citizens Catching a

−37−

Canary:"

> all four were in black, broad-shouldered, tophatted (although for
> some reason one of them was barefoot), and placed in odd, exultant
> and at the same time wary poses beneath the strikingly sunny foli-
> age of a squarely trimmed linden tree in which hid the bird, perhaps
> the one that had escaped from my shoemaker's cage. (58-59; 244)

His description supported by keen eyes that can focus on every detail and
by his imagination works a little miracle in this book, that is, by his transforming the picture into the same language in this text, the border between
the world of Fyodor's reality and that of Romanov's picture waver, allowing
objects belonging to Fyodor's world, for instance, the canary, to enter easily
the space of picture (barefooted man no doubt foreshadows Fyodor, especially his figure in the last chapter).

Romanov gradually matures as an artist, which almost coincides with
Fyodor's maturation. Later in Chapter 3, Fyodor reproduces a "reproduction" of "Footballer" by Romanov, who "had reached full maturity" and "returned to an expressive harmony of line" (181; 361-62). As if he imagined
himself to be Romanov in the process of painting the "pale, sweaty, tensely
distorted face of a player depicted from top to two," Fyodor describes in
detail the player actually "from top to toe," conveying movement, speed
and even sound. He concludes the description with the following comment: "Looking at this picture one could *already* hear the whiz of the
leather missile, *already* see the goalkeeper's desperate dive" (182; 362). Fyodor's description seems to turn the painted player into a real, living person, and even seems to flee the time that is congealed on the surface of the
picture. What should be noted, however, is that the way Fyodor, or more
correctly, Nabokov, translates into words from this painted player seems
practically the same as the way Nabokov describes *his* own character—not
a figure painted in a picture—in the act of playing sport: what might be
recalled here is Humbert's elongated, mesmerizing description of Lolita
playing tennis (*Lo* 230-232). The longish, breathless line describing her

Chapter I Nabokov's Passion for Landscape

serve, in particular, has exactly the same touch and tone as Fyodor's description of the footballer. What Humbert is doing here is to describe the living, moving Lolita as a motionless image in a picture, therefore, the opposite of what Fyodor does. Fyodor here animates the fixed figure in the painting, "turning the picture of a single moment into a narrative of successive actions," while Humbert fixes the animated figure in the real world, turning the active reality into a picture of an arrested moment.[34] In fact, in Nabokov's works there frequently occurs such a moment where the narrator describes a static picture as an animated reality, and an animated reality as a fixed painting. His mastery of translation, therefore, grants his description the specific advantage both of visual art and of narrative art.

Let us again focus on the two works by Romanov. If we read the book carefully, we will notice a curious pattern in common to them: a picture and the world of Fyodor's reality is connected through windows. In the case of the first painting, Fyodor imagines that the painted canary "had escaped from my shoemaker's cage" (59; 244), and we remember that this birdcage is, "although minus its yellow captive, in his [the shoemaker's] purblind window" (57; 242). Here the bird flies out from one frame (the frame of a window) into another frame (that of a picture). The same kind of thing, albeit in less obvious (and less plausible, we have to admit) form, happens to the footballer picture. The window in question could be found in Fyodor's recollection of his classroom, where "the large window was open, sparrows perched on the windowsill and teachers let lessons go by, leaving in their stead squares of blue sky, with footballs falling down out of the blueness" (107; 290). The "squares of blue sky" refers to a succession of views from the open window (so the plural form here does not necessarily

---

[34] The citation is from Heffernan's explanation on one of the features of Homer's ekphrasis, which can be perfectly applicable to Nabokov's case. (Heffernan, James A.W. *Museum of Words: The Poetics of Ekphrasis from Homer to Ashbery.* Chicago: U of Chicago P, 1993, 4)

Reading Nabokov's Framed Landscape

signify more than one window). This simple yet spectacular view of the blue sky and a football in the framed window lingers not only in Fyodor's memory but in the reader's, so we are not inclined to negate the possibility of a certain connection between this window and the picture "Footballer."

As the two cases above show, in Nabokov's world windows and pictures are inseparably connected, sometimes superimposed on each other.[35]

There is another impressive description of a painting, which is, unlike those above, based on a really existing work.[36] In his attempts to describe his father's exploration, Fyodor shows us the picture in detail:

> Among the old, tranquil, velvet-framed family photographs in my father's study there hung a copy of the picture: Marco Polo leaving Venice. She was rosy, this Venice, and the water of her lagoon was azure, with swans twice the size of the boats, into one of which tiny violet men were descending by way of a plank, in order to board a ship which was waiting a little way off with sails furled.... (115-6; 299)

What is ingenious and different from those examples examined above is that when the narrator is describing the picture it is not placed there for him to see: he is recollecting and visualizing the painting as it hung on the past wall and translating it into language. Notwithstanding the fact that Fyodor's verbal reproduction is based on his memory and not by the present real picture, the reader can clearly and freshly visualize it.[37] As always, when the narrator expresses the ongoing drama on the still, motionless

---

[35] Though there are numerous examples, one of the most obvious one is found in *Bend Sinister*: "... the view framed in the casements... was not only a sample of picture of that particular region ..." (*BS* 84); also in *Lolita*, the view from the window of Chestnut Court is depicted, according to Johnson and deVrie, as a kind of Italian painting of the pilgrimage theme (*Art of Painting* 31), but it also recalls the world of Breughel, whose works Nabokov often refers to, though without drawing from any particular piece, for he is only using Breughelian tints and style.

[36] *Art of Painting*, 170.

Chapter I Nabokov's Passion for Landscape

surface of the painting by using the progressive tense ("tiny violet men were descending" and so on), the picture in front of our eyes ceases to be a motionless picture and is transformed into a moving, animated scene. This impression is enhanced by the following remark: "I cannot tear myself away from this mysterious beauty, these ancient colors which swim before the eyes as if seeking new shapes …" (116; 299). This passage magically makes the painted, motionless water of Venice melt into real, rippling water. So we have the impression that the process of translating the picture into words allows a motionless solid image to be restored to its original, that is, real, liquid, moving water. The expression "I cannot tear myself" should also be noted. Although "I," namely, the present, narrating person (Fyodor the narrator), is merely remembering this picture (the actual painting therefore does not exist before his proper eyes), he is able to see it and talk about it as if it was really in front of him. The reader, sharing the special, talented eye of the narrator, experiences an extraordinary moment when solid water on the flat canvas returns to almost real, flowing, scintillating water. Moreover, the narrator says "before the eyes" and not "before my eyes," thus permitting us to read it as the eyes of Fyodor the narrator, of Fyodor the character, and of the reader too.

The character (though he is a real figure and not exactly a character) who is depicted as having quite a different idea of visual art than Nabokov / Fyodor is Nikolai Chernyshevski. In his biography of this historical figure, Fyodor quotes Chernyshevki's verbal description of visual arts from his note about "poetic pictures" exhibited in "the windows of Junker's and Daziaro's" on the Nevski Avenue: "Particularly unsuccessful was the glabella as well as the parts lying near the nose, on both sides of its bridge" (222; 401); "On her knees in a cave, Mary Magdalene was praying before a

---

[37] To describe from memory is, as has been already noted, what Nabokov learnt from Dobzhinski. He sometimes uses this method when describing details from a literary work also.

Reading Nabokov's Framed Landscape

skull and cross, and of course her face in the light of the lampad was very sweet, but how much better was Nadezhda Yegorovna's semi-illumined face!" (223; 401). Chernyshevski takes "comparative method," that is, the purpose of his ekphrasis is to compare the beauty of Nadezhda, a real woman, and the beauty of a woman in pictures. He therefore concludes: "life is more pleasing (and therefore better) than painting" (223; 402). The effect and result of Fyodor's ekphrasis is quite different from Chernyshevski's: by translating a picture into verbal art, Fyodor succeeds in conveying the essence of the picture, in erasing the boundary between two sister arts. In Nabokov's works, therefore, the idea of superiority of one art to the other is rather nonsensical.

Nabokov's works abounds with descriptions of visual art, among which are those of "paintings which positively recalls existing ones but differ markedly from these in some details." [38] There is also a type of painter whom Nabokov never mentions but whose works have a strong affinity in a certain aspect with his works (like an unaccountable, "telepathic" similarity between Nabokov and Borges.[39] A good example of such painters is his coeval Edward Hopper (1882-1967). Alain de Botton, in his work of exquisite literary invitation to a voyage, exhibits certain canvases of Hopper's to show how this American painter found "poetry" in "ignored, often derided landscapes" such as motel rooms, petrol stations, diners and cafeterias.[40] His description of Hopper's paintings and themes, curiously enough, sounds as if it referred to the world of *Lolita*, where Nabokov sketches in detail such roadside facilities as motels, gas stations, soda fountains and so on. They both find poetic inspiration in otherwise prosaic roadside details, almost subliming them as a part of American landscape. Therefore some readers may be inclined to imagine Lolita and Humbert finding Hopper's

---

[38] *Art of Paintings*, 25.
[39] See *Strong Opinions*, 80.
[40] De Botton, Alain. *The Art of Travel*. London: Penguin, 2003, 50.

Chapter I Nabokov's Passion for Landscape

paintings in the *History of Modern American Painting*, which Humbert gave to Lolita as a birthday present (*Lo* 199).

The capital motif that connects the two artists, however, is the window motif. As Hopper obsessively kept painting windows of a café, of a motel, or of a moving train, Nabokov repeatedly depicted scenes with a window. "Views from trains" especially are their common interest.[41] In the next chapter we will examine how these windows work in Nabokov's world.

---

[41] Ibid., 51.

Chapter II
Nabokov through Windowpanes

1. View from a Window

We cannot help noticing a considerable number of windows and views from a window prevailing in the scenes examined in the previous chapter: we had the garden views from colored windowpanes; a replica of the Tamara Gardens behind the glass; the window through which Cincinnatus tries to escape, and so on. Though it is not uncommon for an author to use a window as an artistic device, Nabokov's obsession with the window is highly exceptional. "Windows," says Kinbote in his commentary on John Shade's poem *Pale Fire*, "as well known, have been the solace of first-person literature throughout the ages,"[1] and he mentions Lermontov's *A Hero of Our Time* and Proust's *Time Lost* as examples. Nabokov, also as a commentator of Pushkin's *Eugene Onegin*, noticing repeated appearances of Tatiana by the window, concludes: "Her selenotropic soul is constantly turned toward a romantic remoteness; the window becomes an emblem of yearning and solitude" (*EO* II 282). Curiously enough, however, the window motif has not been fully discussed before now. In this section, we will focus on this unfairly neglected theme—the window theme and especially the theme of window-framed view, scattered throughout Nabokov's works.[2]

First of all we will study several important window scenes found in

---

[1] Nabokov, Vladimir. *Pale Fire*. New York: Vintage, 1989, 87. Henceforth as *PF*.

Chapter II Nabokov through Windowpanes

Speak, Memory. The first paragraph of the autobiography already shows the imagery of a window: a home made film in which "a young chronophobi-ac" catches a glimpse "of his mother waving from an upstairs window, and that unfamiliar gesture disturbed him, as if it were some mysterious fare-well" (*SM* 17). Although this is not a mention of Nabokov's own memory, but is only an imagined scene, the scene strangely lingers on the reader's mind, as the first visual image in this book. In fact, this is "a significant de-tail," Alexandrov points out, "that does not appear in either the two earlier versions of the autobiography."[3] Showing how wrong this chronophobiac's interpretation of the state before birth as a black void is, Nabokov, in the rest of the paragraph, is trying to prove that "the 'abysses' preceding and following human life may not be quite as empty and foreboding as might seem."[4] Nabokov must have added this particular detail of the mother waving from the window with the intention of reinforcing this idea, sug-gesting another interpretation of her action: her waving does not mean "farewell," but a "welcome;" she is seeing him, waving him, recognizing him, already before his birth. The window, therefore, must be here in the opening paragraph of this autobiography: this may be a window opened on "the walls of time separating [him] ... from the free world of timeless-ness" (*SM* 17-8). This first window brilliantly foretells the significant role a number of windows will play through the whole book, allowing windows to be one of the most significant themes in the work.

Now let us return to that scene of Mademoiselle reading on the veran-da. The window here serves as a frame that changes a view into a kind of

---

[2] Kuzmanovich only briefly mentions "Lighted windows" as "metaphors for the work of consciousness, at once a barrier and an opening, a brink." (Kuzmanovich, Zoran. "Strong opinions and nerve points: Nabokov's life and art," in *The Cambridge Companion to Nabokov,* ed. Julian Connolly [Cambridge: Cambridge UP, 2005], 11-30, 19.)

[3] Alexandrov, *Nabokov's Otherworld,* 24.

[4] Ibid., 24.

– 45 –

picture. Later, the old Nabokov recalls the view of the garden as a piece of painting. The readings of Mademoiselle are strongly connected to the memory of those windowpanes. What is stressed in this passage is not the stories she reads but the "potent" rhythm and the nature of her voice. The narrator underscores the potential of "the even flow of her voice" (*SM* 84), explaining how his surroundings (a tree, its leaves, a Comma butterfly, and a wagtail) are borrowing "the rare purity of her rhythmic voice" (*SM* 83). This line has its mirror image in *Lolita*. While describing the "stationary triviality" of a gas station, Humbert Humbert mentions radio music coming from the office: "and because the rhythm was not synchronized with the heave and flutter and other gestures of wind-animated vegetation, one had the impression of an old scenic film living its own life while piano or fiddle followed a line of music quite outside the shivering flower, the swaying branch" (*Lo* 211-12). This incongruity, the gap, between music and scenery, evokes the "sound of Charlotte's last sob" in Humbert's mind.

What is marvelous in this whole passage about the colored windows is that those colored panes through which the child Nabokov peers into the garden imperceptibly change themselves into the windows through which the old Nabokov looks into the past: we experience a rare moment when the eyes of the child and those of the adult Nabokov meet together through the glasses. During that moment Mademoiselle's reading voice is still heard, with the words being devoid of any meaning, far from the book itself, distracting the child's attention to the outer world.

Chapter 5, originally called "Mademoiselle O," if contrasting its neighboring chapter (Chapter 4) named "My English Education," could be subtitled as "My French Education." So the two chapters can be in a certain degree regarded as twins, and indeed the English Education chapter has a scene that might form a pair with the present scene above, that is, a scene marked by the correlation of the window theme and the book motif.

After introducing his "first English friends," four characters in his grammar book ("Ben, Dan, Sam and Ned"), Nabokov describes the room

– 46 –

Chapter II Nabokov through Windowpanes

where he is:

> The schoolroom was drenched with sunlight. In a sweating glass jar,
> several spiny caterpillars were feeding on nettle leaves . . . . The oil-
> cloth that covered the round table smelled of glue. Miss Clayton
> smelled of Miss Clayton. Fantastically, gloriously, the blood-colored
> alcohol of the outside thermometer had risen to 24° Réaumur (86°
> Fahrenheit) in the shade. Through the window one could see ker-
> chiefed peasant girls weeding a garden path on their hands and
> knees or gently raking the sun-mottled sand . . . . Golden orioles in
> the greenery emitted their four brilliant notes: dee-del-dee-O!
>
> Ned lumbered past the window in a fair impersonation of the
> gardener's mate Ivan . . . . (*SM* 63-64)

Here the boy's attention, though in the middle of reading, seems to be di-
rected to the outside the window. Extremely curious is the last remark:
"Ned lumbered past the window." We must remember here that Ned is
one of his imaginary friends in his grammar. So what happens here is that
a fictitious character in a book somehow tumbles out of the "real" window
into the "real" world. We may dare say that this magic moment might be
triggered off by "four brilliant notes" of the golden orioles (dee-del-
dee-O!) as a magic spell. The world of book merges with the world of reality through the medium of window.

Also we notice the crescendo of the sense of certain expectancy: we
cannot help expecting something unusual is going to happen, sensing a
certain excitement under the quiet, calm surface of the passage, especially
by the words "Fantastically, gloriously," and by the increasing warmness indicated on the thermometer. The excitement grows to the highest point
when we hear the Golden orioles cry.

In this scene the window seems to become for a moment the boundary
between this world and the world of fiction. It needs, however, some trigger for a window to turn into the entrance of the otherworld. In the case
of the colored window episode, Mademoiselle's potent and rhythmical

Reading Nabokov's Framed Landscape

voice seems to work as a magic spell to evoke a magic moment (the phrase "Golden orioles in the greenery," with its comfortably repeated "g" and "o," has itself a magical tone); here in the episode of grammar book, the cry of the oriole seems to serve as the immediate trigger for the child to glimpse a fictitious character outside the window.[5]

The combination of window / book is another significant theme, which we will study more closely later.

Another important window found in Chapter 4 is an oriel in his mother's boudoir through which he looks on "the Morskaya in the direction of the Maria Square:" "With lips pressed against the thin fabric that veiled the windowpane I would gradually taste the cold of the glass through the gauze. From that oriel, some years later, at the outbreak of the Revolution, I watched various engagements and saw my first dead man" (*SM* 71). First it must be noted that he begins with a mention of the windowpane itself: before looking at the view through it, he focuses on the glass itself, enjoying fully its presence as a material. More important is the fact that he feels the glass indirectly, through the thin fabric. The veil here seems to serve as a curtain hiding the stage from the expectant audience in the theatre. Moreover, the touch of the line describing his tasting the gradual seep of the texture of the glass even seems to show his special fetish of this windowpane.

This line brilliantly echoes the passage about "the pleasure of handling a certain beautiful, delightfully solid, garnet-dark crystal egg": "I used to chew a corner of the bedsheet until it was thoroughly soaked and then wrap the egg in it tightly, so as to admire and re-lick the warm, ruddy glit-

---

[5] The "dee-del-dee-O!" seems to accidentally predict the arrival of Mademoiselle O, who is, curiously enough, sometimes associated with birds: her only Russian "gde" ("where") is uttered "like the raucous cry of some lost bird" (*SM* 77), while she speaks French with "the nightingale voice" (*SM* 89); towards the end of this Mademoiselle chapter, Nabokov connects the image of "an aged swan" to her (*SM* 92).

– 48 –

Chapter II Nabokov through Windowpanes

ter of the snugly enveloped facets that came seeping through with a miraculous completeness of glow and color" (*SM* 20-21). Being wrapped in the wet sheet, the glow and the color gradually seep through, as if they were a liquid essence of beauty: as the words "feeding upon" suggest, the child Nabokov seems to try to suck the delicious juice, the elixir, of the solid crystal by artistically transforming the nature of its material (liquidating a solid).

The two episodes, sharing the same image of his lip contacting something through a veil, could be more firmly connected and more clearly understood, when compared to a part of the vision the child Nabokov saw during his convalescence from a long illness:

> I watched, too, the familiar pouting movement she [his mother] made to distend the network of her close-fitting veil drawn too tight over her face, and as I write this, the touch of reticulated tenderness that my lips used to feel when I kissed her veiled cheek comes back to me—*flies* back to me with a shout of joy out of the snow-blue, blue-windowed (the curtains are not yet drawn) past. (*SM* 32)

We can infer that this tender touch of his mother's cheek behind the veil that he felt with his lips must be the essential sensation that permeates and connects the two episodes. Both episodes take on a subtly sensual, amorous atmosphere, which is deepened when read together with this rather privileged memory of the kiss on his mother's cheek.

It is worth noting that here the window is used as a metaphor. The touch of "tenderness," as a bird, flies back to the present Nabokov from the past through the window. The window serves as the boundary between present and past: more correctly, the entrance to the world of past opened on the wall of the present room. We could visualize here Nabokov sitting and writing in a many-windowed room; each window shows in it different scene from past world, and if "the curtains are not yet drawn," things can still freely enter from the past world.

– 49 –

The image of the author we have visualized here leads us straight back to the four-line stanza with which Nabokov concludes Foreword of this memoir: "Through the window of that index / Climbs a rose / And sometimes a gentle wind *ex* / Ponto blows" (*SM* 12). *Speak, Memory* has rather an unusual Index (though not as unusual as the Index of *Pale Fire*), and if we regard each index as a window (also "index" and "window" are a perfectly harmonious couple in terms of sound), and open the indicated page, we could see through this window a detailed view in the past. A rose bloomed in the past garden could even climb into the present room through the window.

Now let us go back to that oriel in his mother's boudoir. Besides that tender memory of the glass felt through his lips the window shows him a glimpse of death, and after recollecting this rather tragic scene, he shows how "there was nothing to watch" through this oriel in the days of Mr Burness's (a tutor of his) lessons, save "the dark, muffled street and its receding line of loftily suspended lamps, around which the snowflakes passed and repassed with graceful, almost deliberately slackened motion, as if to show how the trick was done and how simple it was" (*SM* 71). Though it seems that he regards the view as insignificant, the actual description, being highly detailed and impressive, transforms this otherwise trivial, pointless view into something worth description.

This is followed by a typically Nabokovian shift of viewpoints: "From another angle, one might see a more generous stream of snow in a brighter, violet-tinged nimbus of gaslight, and then the jutting enclosure where I stood would seem to drift slowly up and up, like a balloon" (*SM* 71). This paragraph concerning the oriel, therefore, is multi-dimensionally constructed, including the description of the window itself, the outside view through the window, and the picture of the window seen from the outside. This sudden shift of viewpoints is one of the elements that endow the window theme with complexity and richness.

The episode of the oriel window tells us that a window could be a

Chapter II Nabokov through Windowpanes

peephole through which one can get a glimpse of death. The window that vaguely reflects death is found at the end of Chapter 1, in the most significant and already well discussed (though in quite a different context) scene. It begins as follows:

> Several times during a summer it might happen that in the middle of luncheon, in the bright, many-windowed, walnut-paneled dining room on the first floor of our Vyra manor, Aleksey, the butler . . . would bend over and inform my father in a low voice . . . that a group of villagers wanted to see the *barin* outside. (*SM* 26)

With the image "many-windowed" in mind, let us see how those windows work in the following passages. First, "[o]ne of the windows at the west end of the dining room" through which one can see "the top of the honeysuckle bushes opposite the porch," and from that direction "the courteous buzz of a peasant welcome would reach us as the invisible group greeted my invisible father," so he cannot see them and only hears the sound. Next comes into focus another window: "The ensuing parley, conducted in ordinary tones, would not be heard, as the windows underneath which it took place were closed to keep out the heat" (*SM* 26). Nabokov finally describes how "the good barin would be put through the national ordeal of being rocked and tossed up and securely caught by a score or so of strong arms":

> From my place at table I would suddenly see through one of the west windows a marvelous case of levitation. There, for an instant, the figure of my father in his wind-rippled white summer suit would be displayed, gloriously sprawling in midair, his limbs in a curiously casual attitude, his handsome, imperturbable features turned to the sky." (*SM* 26-27)

As the verb "display" suggests, Nabokov shows his father's figure as if it were a framed picture. Moreover, by allowing us to understand the frequency of this scene ("Several times during a summer") through the repeated use of "would," this "marvelous case of levitation" is endowed with an air of eternity, allowing it to continue forever, expressing "the continuity

-51-

of time and its unity," as Nabokov observes in his lecture on Flaubert's *Madame Bovary* (*LL* 173) concerning his special use of the French imperfection form of the past tense. Nabokov says in English *imparfait* is "best rendered by *would* or *used to*" (*LL* 173). In fact, one of special features of Nabokov's style is this very usage of "would," which is most likely influenced by French *imparfait*. We will examine the theme later.

Also Nabokov elongates the last sentence to the utmost, as if he were trying to halt the window-framed picture of the soaring father in midair as long as possible:

> Thrice, to the mighty heaveho of his invisible tossers, he would fly up in this fashion, and the second time he would go higher than the first and then there he would be, on his last and loftiest flight, reclining, as if for good, against the cobalt blue of the summer noon, like one of those paradisiac personages who comfortably soar, with such a wealth of folds in their garments, on the vaulted ceiling of a church while below, one by one, the wax tapers in mortal hands light up to make a swarm minute flames in the mist of incense, and the priest chants of eternal repose, and funeral lilies conceal the face of whoever lies there, among the swimming lights, in the open coffin. (*SM* 27)

The second half of the line shows not a real image but a long simile; however, "whoever lies there" could inevitably be identified with his father. As has been thoroughly discussed, the whole line above prefigures the image of his father's death.[6]

Curiously enough, critics have not focused on the fact that this is a scene framed by a window.[7] The whole section ("5" of Chapter 1) set in

---

[6] Boyd's interpretation of this line is now famous: "Despite the generalized nature of the church scene that materializes beneath the sky's blue vault, Nabokov in fact anticipates here . . . a precise moment later in his own life, the day he looks down at his father lying in an open coffin." See Boyd, Brian. *Vladimir Nabokov. The Russian Years*, Princeton: Princeton UP, 1990, 7.

the "many-windowed dining room" is quite orderly constructed, focusing on one window after another, with different scene displayed in each in such a way that the scenes are shown as on a roll of film.

The last window here thus serves as a boundary between this world and "otherworld," as that oriel window when it shows Nabokov his first dead man. What makes this scene one of the most memorable one is, perhaps, this window: this rare moment is caught, framed and preserved by this window, staying long in one's mind as a picture. A window becomes sometimes a boundary and other times serves to change a transient sight into a durable, picture-like view.

2. Train Windows

The window motif develops into the theme of train window, which also pervades Nabokov's works. Trains themselves are "one of the most insistent of the many leitmotifs in the autobiography,"[8] and it is essential to notice that the train theme is frequently entwined with the window theme. The first evocation of this image in *Speak, Memory* is in Chapter 1, after the episode of the "garnet-dark crystal egg" we have already examined, where he fondly describes his "earliest impressions" which "led the way to a veritable Eden of visual and tactile sensations":

> One night, during a trip abroad, in the fall of 1903, I recall kneeling on my (flattish) pillow at the window of a sleeping car ... and seeing with an inexplicable pang, a handful of fabulous lights that beckoned to me from a distant hillside, and then slipped into a

---

[7] Akikusa, however, in his precise reading of this scene, pays attention to the windows and aptly calls this many-windowed room "a room without view." 秋草俊一郎 「ナボコフが付けなかった注釈：ナボコフ訳注『エヴゲーニー・オネーギン』を貫く政治的姿勢について」Slavistika XXIII 東京大学大学院人文社会学科研究科, 2007. 77

[8] Alexandrov, *Otherworld*, 48.

Reading Nabokov's Framed Landscape

pocket of black velvet: diamonds that I later gave away to my characters to alleviate the burden of my wealth. (*SM* 21)

As one of the "first thrills" that "belong to the harmonious world of a perfect childhood" (*SM* 21), this memory of his favorite keeps feeding rich images of train windows to his works.

The first section of Chapter 7 of *Speak, Memory*, independently published as a short story under the title of "First Love," consists of a dazzling sequence of views from the "then great and glamorous Nord Express" (*SM* 111). More correctly, some of them are not necessarily a view but a reflection, as the very first case shows. Nabokov represents a reflected image of the nine-year-old Nabokov and his mother playing a card game: "Although it was still broad daylight, our cards, a glass and, on a different plane, the locks of a suitcase were reflected in the window. Through forest and field, and in sudden ravines, and among scuttling cottages, those discarnate gamblers kept steadily playing on for steadily sparkling stakes" (*SM* 112). What is remarkable is the smooth shift of the glasses that follows:

> . . . on this gray winter morning, in the looking glass of my bright hotel room, I see shining the same, the very same, locks of that now seventy-year-old valise, a highish, heavyish *nécessaire de voyage* of pigskin, with "H.N." elaborately interwoven in thick silver under a similar coronet, which had been bought in 1897 for my mother's wedding trip to Florence. (*SM* 112)

What happens here is that the glass of a train window in the past dissolves into a looking glass in the hotel room where the present Nabokov is writing this. Therefore the eyes of the child are suddenly replaced by those of the old Nabokov.[9]

The next window shows us the repeated rise and fall of the "six thin

---

[9] "H.N." is the reflected figure of the Russian "И.Н" that stands for Irina Nabokov, the name of Nabokov's mother. Suitcase is another important motif in Nabokov's works.

−54−

Chapter II Nabokov through Windowpanes

black wires": they "were doing their best to slant up, to ascend skywards, despite the lightning blows dealt them by one telegraph pole after another; but just as all six, in a triumphant swoop of pathetic elation, were about to reach the top of the window, a particularly vicious blow would bring them down, as low as they had ever been, and they would have to start all over again" (*SM* 113). This recurrent movement shown in the window seems to be subtly imitated in the child's mind by the wave of the ocean, in the third and the last section: "One strange night, I lay awake, listening to the recurrent thud of the ocean and planning our [the child Nabokov's and Colette's] flight. The ocean seemed to rise and grope in the darkness and then heavily fall on its face" (*SM* 118).

Incidentally, section 1 is reflected in the last section in an elaborate manner. The most obvious reflection is the imagery of a glass marble. In his sleep in the sleeping car, he sees "a glass marble rolling under a grand piano or a toy engine lying on its side with its wheels still working gamely" (*SM* 114). Towards the end of the chapter, the narrator remembers "some detail in her [Colette's] attire (perhaps a ribbon on her Scottish cap, or the pattern of her stockings) that reminded me then of the rainbow spiral in a glass marble" (*SM* 119). Another noticeable motif in common is a "minia-ture," or a "replica." This chapter begins with the recollection of "a three-foot-long model of an oak-brown international sleeping car" displayed in a travel agency on Nevski Avenue (most likely in the shop window). The eye of the narration (a combined eye of the narrator and the child) comes gradually closer to the replica, peering through the car window, making out the "maddening details" inside. He does not forget mentioning how the windows look like: "Spacious windows alternated with narrower ones, single or geminate, and some of these were of frosted glass" (*SM* 111). The corresponding image in the third section is "a miraculous photographic view of the bay and of the line of cliffs ending in a lighthouse" seen through "a tiny peephole of crystal" set in a penholder (*SM* 119). The two miniatures and also the image of the peering eye through a glass (a glass of

−55−

the shop window, small train windows, and the crystal eyehole) cleverly adorn the entrance and the exit of this short story.[10] This could be categorized, of course, in the variants of the window theme, and we could even say that a glass marble and its spiral inside may be a deformed image of a windowpane and the view through it.

The corridor window with its view of the six wires is followed by another spectacular, kaleidoscopic show involving almost all the windows. He explains "a twofold excitement" felt when the train passes through "some big German town" (*SM* 113). First he sees "a city, with its toylike trams, linden trees and brick walls, enter the compartment, hobnob with the mirrors, and fill to the brim the windows on the corridor side."[11] The other excitement is derived through the act of "putting myself in the place of some passer-by." The child Nabokov imagines this passer-by is "moved as I would be moved myself to see the long, romantic, auburn cars, with their intervestibular connecting curtains as black as bat wings and their metal lettering copper-bright in the low sun, unhurriedly negotiate an iron bridge across an everyday thoroughfare and then turn, with all windows suddenly ablaze, around a last block of houses" (*SM* 113). One observes here again the highly Nabokovian shift of viewpoints, which occurs in the aforementioned episode of the oriel window in his mother's boudoir. This shift has also much to do with Nabokov's famous "cosmic synchroniza-

---

[10] He explains his love for miniatures or a compact world reduced in a glass frame when talking about the loveliness of the printed landscapes on the glass slides for a lantern-slide ("translucent miniature, pocket wonderlands, neat little worlds of hushed luminous hues!") and "the same precise and silent beauty at the radiant bottom of a microscope's magic shaft": "There is, it would seem, in the dimensional scale of the world a kind of delicate meeting place between imagination and knowledge, a point, arrived at by diminishing large things and enlarging the small ones, that is intrinsically artistic" (*SM* 130-31).

[11] To "hobnob with the mirrors" reminds us (and inevitably the author too) of the image of a moth. Cf., the moth that "hobnobbed with its own shadow" on the ceiling in "Cloud, Castle, Lake."

Chapter II Nabokov through Windowpanes

tion," or "multilevel thinking," by which Nabokov means "the capacity of thinking of several things at a time," which also "appears one of characteristic traits of all of his positive characters."[12] This special way of thinking is based on the ability to perceive several objects from different points of view at the same time, sometimes implying the ability to putting oneself in another's place, which is what the boy in the train is doing here.[13]

Another impressive image of a landscape is an imagined, "illegible," one at night behind the blinded window. Although the paragraph in question has no mention of windows at all, one could well imagine the dark windows and the "headlong rush of the outside night" (*SM* 114). We will be amazed to find how elaborately this paragraph is constructed with the theme of "letters" (or "words"). It begins as follows: "It was at night, however, that the *Compagnie Internationale des Wagons-Lits et des Grands Express Européens* lived up to the magic of its name" (*SM* 114). One can imagine that the name above may be written on the body of each car, for a passer-by on the street could recognize the "metal lettering copper-bright in the low sun." The reader, therefore, is expected to visualize this rather long name painted on the side of the train. The narrator describes rather calm, almost stationary objects inside the car and then concludes the paragraph with the image of the contrasting "headlong rush of the outside night, which I knew *was* rushing by, spark-streaked, illegible" (*SM* 114), the choice of "illegible" not only conveying the degree to which the nocturnal landscape is merely glimpsed through the window of the rushing train, but also conferring on the scenery the sense of it as a written text: a landscape as something to be read. At the same time, there is one more thing which must be illegible now and which this adjective suits better than the night view. If we use "cosmic synchronization" here and try to see

---

[12] Alexandrov, *Otherworld*, 27.

[13] Fyodor in *The Gift* is bequeathed with this gift too, with his special talent of putting himself in another's place.

the rushing train from outside, we could see that magically long name on the train body speeding by and completely illegible. More interesting is that now this long lettering "*Compagnie Internationale des Wagons-Lits et des Grands Express Européens*" on the text looks really like the long train itself, which is possibly a part of "the magic of its name."

Nabokov indeed sometimes shows us a landscape as a readable text, translating it into language for his reader, especially when he describes the view from a moving vehicle. More interestingly, reading landscape from a car window is sometimes in contrast to reading a book there. Vasiliy Ivanovich in "Cloud, Castle, Lake," not permitted by his fellow passengers to read his favourite book on the train, tries to find something interesting in the landscape through the window instead. Gifted with special eyesight, he can read the passing landscape carefully and in detail, being even able to focus on a stationary object among the fast moving surroundings. Another interesting passage showing this contrast is found in Fyodor's biography of Nikolay Gavrilovich Chernyshevski, in which he depicts the hero reading in a carriage and the "unnoticed" landscape:

> . . . the landscape which not long before had with wondrous languor unfolded along the passage of the immortal *brichka*; all that Russian viatic lore, so untrammeled as to bring tears to the eyes; all the humbleness that gazes from the field, from a hillock,
>
> from between oblong clouds; that suppliant, expectant beauty which is ready to rush toward you at the slightest sigh and share your tears; in short, the landscape hymned by Gogol passed unnoticed before the eyes of the eighteen-year-old Nikolay Gavrilovich, who with his mother was traveling in a carriage drawn by their own horses from Saratov to St. Petersburg. The whole way he kept reading a book. It goes without saying that he preferred his "war of words" to the "corn ears bowing in the dust." (214; 393)

What is remarkable is the way Fyodor sums up the landscape: by saying "the landscape hymned by Gogol," the author shows the landscape itself as

Chapter II Nabokov through Windowpanes

something described in a literary text. Chernyshevski's book, however, swallows this poetical view. The author concludes this journey with the duplicated image of the surroundings and the text Chernyshevski reads: "... and a hole in the road loses its meaning of hole, becoming merely a typographical unevenness, a jump in the line—and now again the words pass evenly by, the trees pass by and their shadow passes over the pages" (216; 395). To Chernyshevski whose "blindness" Fyodor keeps mentioning, landscape from a moving vehicle does not exist, and this blindness also leads to his "deficiency of botanical knowledge" and makes him maintain that the flowers of Siberian taiga "are all just the same as those which bloom all over Russia" (244; 422). His philosophy, Fyodor says, is constructed "on a basis of knowing the world" (244; 422), so he might think there is nothing new and extraordinary to see in the nature out of the window. It is true the view from the carriage goes invisible to him, but he enjoys the view of St. Petersburg from his window. In the mornings he "would open his window and ... would cross himself facing the shimmering glitter of the cupolas: St. Isaac's, in the process of construction, was all in scaffolding" (216; 395). He also "had actually seen a train" (216; 395), but in Fyodor's biography he never takes one, thus not allowed to see wonderful views from the train window that Nabokov (and perhaps Fyodor also) so loved. St. Isaac's, incidentally, could be seen from a window of Nabokov's house, and possibly Fyodor's house too, so Fyodor, while writing this, must see this view clearly (in his mind), regarding this window as his own window. Indeed, the image of Chernyshevski looking out of the window with the view of St. Isaac's under construction recalls a capital window scene at the beginning of this novel, which we will closely examine later in the next section.

Chernyshevski's attitude toward a landscape seen from a moving vehicle forms a singular contrast to Vasiliy Ivanovich's in "Cloud, Castle, Lake." To compare them thoroughly, let us first clarify how beautifully the window theme is working in this story.

–59–

Reading Nabokov's Framed Landscape

We must now remember the room that is so ideal for Vasiliy Ivanovich. The room itself "had nothing remarkable about it," but "from the window one could clearly see the lake with its cloud and its castle, in a motionless and perfect correlation of happiness." He realizes that "here in this little room with that view . . . life would at last be what he had always wished it to be" (*Stories* 435). It is only by staying in this room that Vasiliy Ivanovich can possess this view of the lake, its cloud and its castle as his own. The cloud itself is no one's, nor is the castle itself, but they are represented as a part of the lake; while the lake itself, if seen from the room, becomes a part of the room (or the window), thus a belonging of the observer. Vasiliy Ivanovich on the one hand has a keen appreciation of the beauty of a landscape seen through the window of a fast moving train, but on the other has a desire to "arrest moment," a desire for "a fixed location, in a stable vision of order and harmony."[14] The following quotation, which forms a striking contrast to the description of Chernyshevski's blind ride, shows this precisely:

> We both, Vasiliy Ivanovich and I, have always been impressed by the anonymity of all the parts of a landscape, so dangerous for the soul, the impossibility of ever finding out where that path you see leads—and look, what a tempting thicket! It happened that on a distant slope or in a gap in the tree there would appear and, as it were, stop for an instant, like air retained in the lungs, a spot so enchanting—a lawn, a terrace—such perfect expression of tender well-meaning beauty—that it seemed that if one could stop the train and go thither, forever, to you, my love . . . But a thousand beech trunks were already madly leaping by, whirling in a sizzling sun pool, and again the chance for happiness was gone. (*Stories* 432)

The narrator's long, breathless line itself seems to express the almost non-stop movement of the train, and the hero's desire to "stop" every move-

---

[14] Shawen, "Motion and Statis," 381.

−60−

Chapter II Nabokov through Windowpanes

ment. A whirling landscape cannot give him a desirable peace, but the view of "the motionless and unchanging lake" can. Then why does he need a stable, stationary location? It is not only a matter of longing for "victories over times and space."[15]

To fully understand Vasiliy's attitude it is essential to notice the problem of "ownership" underlying the story. When we read it carefully, we will note the narrator's rather persistent usage of the possessive. First of all he introduces Vasiliy to us as "one of my representatives" (*Stories* 430), the exact meaning of which remains vague to the end; when his narrative becomes impassioned during descriptions about an idyllic, nostalgic landscape, he cannot help uttering "my love" (*Stories* 432, 434, 435); as has been mentioned, the cloud and the castle are rendered as belongings of the lake ("the lake with its cloud and its castle"). Also the following remark underscores the significance of the "possession" theme:

> In a moment he figured out how he would manage it so as not to have to return to Berlin again, how to get the few possessions that he had—books, the blue suit, her photograph. How simple it was turning out! As my representative, he was earning enough for the modest life of a refugee Russian. (*Stories* 436)

His present possessions are those three above, parallel to the trio of cloud, castle, lake. Vasiliy, a refugee Russian in Berlin, wants to have something truly, eternally his own, which cannot be lost in any way. A passing, transient landscape cannot be possessed by anyone, which keeps in it its "anonymity," thus free of naming and ownership, or authorship (incidentally, both the narrator and "his" hero are, in a way, anonymous, for "Vasiliy" may not be his real name as the narrator admits). However, the stable landscape, especially when framed in a window and so becomes a part of the room, can he own. He could be the owner of the room that owns the view of the lake that owns a cloud and a castle. Not realizing his dream, howev-

---

[15] Shawen, "Motion and Statis," 381.

er, he returns to Berlin and visits the narrator, and, "putting his hands on his knees, told his story" (*Stories* 437). We again come across another trio of his possessions, among which the most important is "his story." Here it turns out finally that the narrator has been recounting "his," Vasiliy Ivanovich's, story, on his behalf: such being the case, Vasiliy's position as a "representative" of the narrator becomes questionable. It seems more reasonable to regard the narrator as Vasiliy's representative, who tells his story for him. The problem of ownership, therefore, is extended even to the matter of who owns this story.

The view from a train window thus yields generous amount of keys to fully enjoy Nabokov's works. Now let us go back to the beginning of this section and share again with the child Nabokov that night view from the train window: the little boy, unlike Chernyshevski and even Vasiliy Ivanovich, could manage to be an owner of these "diamonds" in the velvet night. However, like Vasiliy who "must resign his position" (*Stories* 437), Nabokov readily resigns his ownership and "gave away to my characters to alleviate the burden of my wealth."

3. Fyodor's Windows

As has been briefly mentioned above, the image of Chernyshevski looking out of the window with the view of St. Isaac's under construction recalls the first and the most important window scene at the beginning of this novel. Also Vasiliy Ivanovich's ideal room with a view is firmly linked to the conception of Fyodor's room with a view. In this section we will study the window theme focusing on *The Gift*, especially on Fyodor the protagonist's perception of window views.

The first window scene in *The Gift* is where the narrator describes Fyodor's new, unfamiliar abode and then shifts the focus to what Fyodor sees from his window:

For some time he stood by the window. In the curds-and-whey sky

Chapter II Nabokov through Windowpanes

opaline pits now and then formed where the blind sun circulated,
and, in response, on the gray convex roof of the van, the slender
shadows of linden branches hastened headlong toward substantia-
tion, but dissolves without having materialized. The house directly
across the way was half enclosed in scaffolding, while the sound part
of its brick façade was overgrown with window-invading ivy. At the
far end of the path that cut through its front yard he could make
out the black sign of a coal cellar. (7; 195)
The passage quoted above, though in a way parallel with the scene where
Chernyshevski sees from his window the church in scaffolding, is quite
unique in its unusual detail. Unlike poor-sighted Chernyshevski, Fyodor's
eyes perceive what others cannot perceive, in a highly singular way. Actually, to our common eyes there seems to be nothing worth noticing here in
this view, but his unconventional perception of color ("curds-and-whey,"
"opaline"), his interpretation of the relationship between "the blind sun"
and responding "slender shadows of linden branches," and his curious attention to "window-invading ivy" that excitingly suggests the presence of
another window facing his own, make this view inscrutably significant.
The following remark by the narrator suggests the significance of the
theme of view from a room in this novel: "Taken by itself, all this was a
view, just as the room was itself a separate entity; but now a middleman
had appeared, and now that view became the view from this room and no
other. The gift of sight which it now had received did not improve it" (7-8;
195). The room itself is said to be gifted with sight, which means, it shares
with Fyodor his special eyesight. Through the eyesight of "a middleman,"
that is, Fyodor, the view and the room (or the window) are connected; otherwise these two are totally separate, unrelated things. By his eyesight, the
window of his room owns the view, as if all those one can see through it
belonged to this window: This conception is what connects Vasiliy Ivanovich's room and Fyodor's.[16]
    This idea of the window having its own eyesight is linked to another

−63−

Reading Nabokov's Framed Landscape

theme, the theme of blindness. The opposite of Fyodor's clear-sighted window might be, for example, an old shoemaker's "purblind window" (57; 243) and also that ivy-invaded window opposite his room. The Russian original does not have a correspondent adjective to "purblind," so it is inferable that Nabokov added it for the English version for good reason, to make a contrast to Fyodor's window and to connect this window with the theme of blindness.

To confirm Nabokov's inclination for using this image, let us take a look at another "purblind window," which appears in his short story "The Return of Chorb" (1925).[17] It is not exactly a window but a "black, purblind house," where Chorb stays. The Russian original this time goes "*podslepovatyi dom*,"[18] that is, "purblind house." In Russian this is a common expression, referring to a house with small, or not very clear (not quite transparent), windows, so Nabokov might derive the English "purblind window" from the Russian usage of the words. Later in the most fascinating scene in this story this purblind window plays an important role, granting the prostitute inside Chorb's room a glimpse of otherworld:

... she ... drew aside the window curtain. Behind the curtain the casement was open and one could make out, in the velvety depth, a corner of the opera house, the black shoulder of a stone Orpheus outlined against the blue of the night, and a row of light along dim façade which slanted off into darkness. Down there, far away, diminutive dark silhouettes swarmed .... (*Stories* 153)

Her point of view "constructs Chorb's room as the space of the living, while the dark streets below are the space of the dead. The text emphasizes

---

[16] Moreover, Vasiliy's first impression of the inn already promises its potential eyesight: "a piebald two-storied dwelling with a winking window beneath a convex tailed eyelids" (*Stories* 435).

[17] Nabokov, Vladimir. "The Return of Chorb." *Stories*, 147-54.

[18] Nabokov, Vladimir. "Vozvraschenie Chorba." *Sobranie sochinenii russkogo perioda v 5 Tomakh*, T1. St. Peterburg: Symposium, 2004, 171.

− 64 −

Chapter II Nabokov through Windowpanes

("down there, far away") the location of Chorb's Hades behind the statue of Orpheus."[19] So here again the window becomes a boundary between "the space of the living" and "the space of the dead."

Also in Fyodor's streets there are "blind houses," by which the narrator means houses with dark windows at night (53; 239), but the expression also implies, no doubt, one's inability to see inside the window: thus "blind" signifies both the window's blindness and that of the one who tries to see it. In other words, "the beholder and what he beholds merge into one"[20]: if you are blind to something, that something is also considered to be blind.[21]

A "blind window" is actually one of many other inanimate objects that the narrator personifies—to put it more precisely, objects endowed with an eye by the narrator. In her collection of optical images in the novel, Berdjis underlines "the importance of visual perception," and we notice there still remain a generous amount of eye motifs, especially blind objects, which she does not fully mention, to add.[22] We will be surprised to know how many eager eyes are trying to open and see in this novel—this is itself in a sense "a long story about a romantic adventure in the town of a hundred eyes, beneath skies unknown" (93; 276). The theme of sight / blind is closely connected to the window theme, so it is necessary to discuss it a little more fully before going back to the window theme.

---

[19] Shrayer, *The World of Nabokov's Stories*, 97.

[20] Berdjis, Nassim Winnie. *Imagery in Vladimir Nabokov's Last Russian Novel* (Дар), *Its English Translation* (The Gift), *and Other Prose Works of the 1930s.* Frankfurt: Peter Lang, 1995, 249.

[21] We have come across several window scenes where the two directions of the eye (the eye turning to the window from inside the room, or the eye of the window itself, and the eye turning to the window from outside the room) could be perceived at the same time. This is really a pivotal idea that constitutes Nabokov's world. If there is a window, we are expected to imagine two beholders: one seeing from inside and one seeing from outside.

[22] Berdjis, *Imagery*, Chapter 5.

A first-rate image of an eye appears as early as in the third paragraph of the novel in the form of a seemingly subsidiary comment in parenthesis on "hanging droplets of rain" among the linden twigs: "(tomorrow each drop would contain a green pupil)" (4; 192) while relating a story of Yasha Chernyshevski, Fyodor represents pine branches, drizzle (48;234), and even "the stroke of drawn lots" (47; 234) as blind; Fyodor tries on a "narrow shoe" in the shop, and his foot when "fitted inside ..., went completely blind" (64; 249). Incidentally, the image of a foot fitted inside a shoe inevitably recalls Fyodor's special trick of pretending to be someone, or "incarnation" (63; 248), in which "his soul would fit snugly into the other's soul" (36; 222). Unlike his blinded toe, Fyodor can "feel a change in the color of his eyes, and also in the color behind his eyes" (63; 248). The blind foot also echoes a remark (albeit imagined one) of Koncheyev on the naked Fyodor: "when one sits next to a naked man one is physically aware that there exist men's outfitters, and one's body feels blind .... But thought likes curtains and the camera obscura" (338; 513). This is also, definitely, a part of the window theme. "Blind sun" is also a familiar expression in the novel.[23] There appear also several blind persons as a comparison, in a figurative sentence : Fyodor "could touch and recognize all of her[Russia] with his soles, as a blind man feels with his palms" (63; 249) (this somewhat reminds us of the child Nabokov who feels and recognizes now invisible path with his forefinger); there is a fence "made out of another one which had been dismantled somewhere else" but "the boards had been placed in senseless order, as if nailed together by a blind man" (176; 356);[24] "To the blind man at the church door" Fyodor's picturesque poems "would have nothing to say" (27; 213); there is also a blind woman to make a pair with a blind man: among a lot of paths leading to Fyodor's house there is a straight

---

[23] If we dare call Fyodor heliotropic (he loves to bathe in the sun, and in the epiphany scene in Grunewalt the sun in a sense transforms Fyodor), Koncheyev, his fellow poet, on the other hand, would be called shade-lover.

Chapter II Nabokov through Windowpanes

avenue, "slim and sleek with a sensitive shadow (rising like a blind woman to meet you and touch your face)" (79; 262-63);[25] in the crucial dream where Fyodor's dead father comes back, "blind children wearing dark spectacles came out of a school building in pairs and walked past him" (353; 528), and the possible source of these blind children in a dream could be discovered in the real world, in the evening before he has this dream: on the street, "a blind man" with a concertina asks Fyodor for alms, and after this two school boys shout at him, riding past (346; 521). Their combined image might create the blind children in his dream. What is interesting is that the only "real" blind character in this novel (a blind man with a concertina) really seems to be able to see things, for he manages to sense Fyodor's presence there in spite of the fact that he, being bare-foot, thus makes no sound. He might not be blind at all, but Fyodor reasons differently (in parenthesis, as when he foresees the eye created in each raindrop): "(it was odd, though—surely he must have heard that I was barefoot)" (346; 521). Here, the visual and auditory senses seem to merge, and this idea of mixed senses is another significant theme in this novel, related to the protagonist's synesthetic nature.[26]

The following is one of the most Nabokovian and as such most noteworthy images of eyesight:

On yesterday's vacant lot a small villa was being built, and since the sky was looking in through the gaps of future windows, and since burdocks and sunlight had taken advantage of the slowness of the

---

[24] The original of the dismantled and blindly reassembled boards are found in Nabokov's memoir: "Animals had been painted on it by a versatile barker; but whoever had removed the boards, and then knocked them together again, must have been blind or insane, for now the fence showed only disjointed parts of animals . . ." (*SM* 172). Here Nabokov seems to compare his blindness as a young poet with this imagined blind man.

[25] The pair motif is also common in Nabokov's works.

[26] See, for example, the section "Synesthesia" in Berdjis's *Imagery*, 145-49.

-67-

work to make themselves comfortable within the unfinished white walls, these had acquired the pensive cast of ruins, like the word "sometime," which serves both the past and the future. (329; 504) The theme of "under construction" is everywhere in Nabokov's works, among which this may be the most suggestive, reminding us of the process by which Fyodor's work of art itself is constructed.[27] Here the eye of the sky is looking into the still absent windows, inside of which the sunlight and burdocks play comfortably, taking advantage of "the slowness of the work." This imperfect house, which is empty but clear-sighted (as the opposite of a "blind house"), reminds us of a "good, thick old-fashioned novel" that Fyodor dreams of writing. Like this villa, the novel seems to be slowly taking shape, and he even likens it to a house, saying "it must be built up, curtained, surrounded by dense life—my life" (364; 539), but he will "be a long time preparing it, years perhaps" (364; 539); at the same time it may have already be written, "because somebody within him, on his behalf, independently from him, had absorbed all this, recorded it, and filed it away" (4; 192). Therefore, like this timeless (containing the nature both of the past and of the present) house, his book is also timeless: *The Gift* itself, as the majority of critics believe, may be the one, thus it was already finished "sometimes" in the past, but at the same time the book will be written "sometime" in the future. Also, the house's "unfinished white wall" echoes a conversation between Zina and Fyodor: "When I [Zina] was little I didn't like drawing anything that didn't finish . . . . I always did something complete, a pyramid, or a house on a hill." "And I liked horizons most of all . . ." (192; 372). This is followed by that discussion on "the white crayon pencil." Therefore, it seems that "unfinished white wall," including both of his favorite—"white" and "incomplete," embodies Fyodor's

---

[27] Dolinin suggests the possibility that "the villa being built on 'yesterday's vacant lot' denotes the novel itself growing out of yesterday's poem and, therefore, out of the author's personal experience" (*Garland Companion* 156).

Chapter II Nabokov through Windowpanes

feeling of what art should be. Finally, the eye of the sky may be interpreted as a reader's eye, or, the author's eye (that is, Nabokov's eye): here the all-looking sky seems to herald, or even to be almost parallel with, the sun image in the following scene in Grunewalt, where it could be considered as "an emblem of a higher authorial consciousness—that which is responsible for creating the character Fyodor."[28]

As the description of the house above and several other images suggest, the theme of sight / blindness and the window theme go together. Now we can return to the main theme. At the end of Chapter 2, Fyodor is leaving (forever) his old residence in Number Seven Tannenberg Street to the new one in 15 Agamemnonstrasse. The narrator suddenly changes his intonation here and turns directly to the reader ("Have you ever happened, reader, to feel that subtle sorrow of parting with an unloved abode?") and thoroughly describes for us "one's" (not "Fyodor's" nor "my") feeling toward the objects in the room and toward the room itself when he is parting with it, and at last he shifts to the first-person voice ("I lived here exactly two years") (144; 327). Immediately before the narrator takes on Fyodor the character's voice, he again mentions the view from the window—the one we examined at the beginning:

> This already dead inventory will not be resurrected later in one's memory: the bed will not follow us, shouldering its own self; the reflection in the dresser will not rise from its coffin; only the view from the window will abide for a while, like the faded photograph, fitted into a cemetery cross, of a trim-haired, steady-eyed gentleman in a starched collar. (144; 327)

Now the window-framed view is compared to a framed, faded picture of a dead person: this man, the personified view, is looking into the room and trying to gaze at someone with his still steady eye, only to find the room

---

[28] Connolly, Julian. *Nabokov's Early Fiction: Patterns of Self and Other.* Cambridge: Cambridge UP, 1992, 212.

−69−

empty, with no eyes for his own to focus on (as every eye in every portrait is wont to focus on your eye. In an empty room their forsaken eyes must keep swimming until someone enters the room and sees them). Therefore, this passage suggests that when Fyodor's room is endowed with sight at the beginning of this novel, the view from the window also gains an eye, so that the inside of the room and the outside view from the window look at each other, play with each other, as that "informal contact between train and city" by means of windows (*SM* 113).

We are also inclined to associate the dead man in the photograph with Fyodor's dead father: although he says he knows that he "will never look in here again" (145; 327), he visits the room once again in his dream, where he reunites with his father. Curiously enough, the first thing Fyodor's eye catches on the threshold between the fading dream and reality is the curtain of his window:

> At first the superposition of a thingummy on a thingabob and the pale, palpitating stripe that went upwards were utterly incomprehensible . . . . But something in his brain turned, his thoughts settled and hastened to paint over the truth—and he realized that he was looking at the curtain of a half-opened window, at a table in front of the window. (355; 530).

This window is not even "his" window but "a" window, and the table is not "his" but "a" table, as if he saw them for the first time. Here, therefore, the realistic, vivid dream world almost conquers the "real" world and transforms it into an unreal, unfamiliar place. In a way he comes back to his now unreal "reality" through this window, so, together with that window looking like a photograph of a dead person, the image of a window becomes a sign to show us the presence of different world, the world of dream, the world of the dead, or whatever.

Moreover, the expression "to paint over the truth" inevitably makes the reader aware of the parallel of this passage and the scene in *Invitation to a Beheading* where Cincinnatus "realized that he was in the very thick of the

– 70 –

Chapter II Nabokov through Windowpanes

Tamara Gardens" and "restored the painting" by removing and erasing the superfluous elements from the surroundings "so as to make them exactly as they were in his memory" (*IB* 187). Both heroes do practically the same thing: suddenly realizing where they really are and finding disunion between what they see and what they remember it is, they try to change the truth based on their memory.

The last scene of Chapter 2 where Fyodor is leaving his old room, leaving the view from the window "abide" for a while, is also reflected in the ending of the novel itself. Fyodor repeats his greeting "good-by" to his room (144; 327), which echoes the narrator's cry "Good-by, my book!" in the last paragraph (366; 541). The narrator's next remark "Like mortal eyes, imagined ones must close some day," therefore, must be parallel with the image of steady-eyed gentleman, the personified view from the window. Also the following passage is remindful of the view that "will abide for a while" after Fyodor leaves: "Onegin from his knees will rise—but his creator strolls away. And yet the ear cannot right now part with the music and allow the tale to fade" (366; 541). As the view abides for a while, the music will abide for a while after the book ends (seems to end). So here again a book is vaguely liken to a house. Another interesting image of a house-like book is the following, referring to the collection of Fyodor's poems: "and now the book lay on the table, completely enclosed within itself, delimited and concluded, and no longer did it radiate those former powerful, glad rays" (55-56; 241). This may be understood as a locked, "blind" house with dark windows, therefore, presents a striking contrast to that never-completed villa with "unfinished white wall." The cover of his book *Poems* is also "creamy white" (6; 194). Later, in Chapter 3, Fyodor unexpectedly sees a copy of this volume again, this time "hidden in a pink cover" by the hand of Zina and looks "quite new to him" (179; 360). This somewhat reminds us of a completely changed house seen from a person who once lived there. When Fyodor's mother visits him in Berlin, they "went to have a look at the apartment house where the three of them [Fyo-

dor, his mother and his sister Tanya] had lived for two years, but the jani-
tor had already changed, the former proprietor had died, strange curtains
hung in the familiar windows, and somehow there was nothing their
hearts could recognize" (90; 273). Zina's pink cover, therefore, could be regarded as an unfamiliar curtain adorning Fyodor's white, old house-like
book. Humbert Humbert experiences a similar situation when he revisits
Ramsdale: "Should I enter my old house? As in a Turgenev story, a tor-
rent of Italian music came from an open window—that of the living room:
what romantic soul was playing the piano where no piano had plunged
and plashed on that bewitched Sunday with the sun on her beloved legs?"
(*Lo* 288) Again the window is a useful device to develop a story.

Let us return to the end of Chapter 2, where Fyodor says farewell to
his room. In the last paragraph the narrator (and Fyodor) gives a final
glance at the window—first at the windowpane itself and then at the view
through it: "A fly climbed up the windowpane, impatiently slipped, half
fell and half flew downwards, as if shaking something, and started to crawl
again. The house opposite, which he had found in scaffolding the April
before last, was evidently in need of repairs again now . . . ." (145; 327).
This is one of the window scenes where one is conscious of the presence of
a window itself (another remarkable example is the oriel window that the
child Nabokov feels through the gauze curtain). The window here is transparent and one can see through it, as if there was nothing between one's
eyes and the view. For the fly, however, the window does exist as nothing
but a solid wall, thus the window sometimes becomes an emblem of something invisible but really existing.[29]

In the last scene of Chapter 2, therefore, the narrator displays three levels of perception of the window: the view looking inside the room from

---

[29] Another deceived creature by the window is "the waxwing slain / By the false azure
in the windowpane" (*PF* 33). The first stanza of the poem *Pale Fire* is a perfect example
to show how the world is multiplied by the presence of a window.

Chapter II Nabokov through Windowpanes

the window, the windowpane itself, and the outside view seen from the inside. As has been noted before, this multiple perception is connected to "multilevel thinking." Fyodor's idea reads as follows:

> ... you look at a person and you see him as clearly as if he were fashioned of glass and you were a glass blower, while at the same time without impinging upon that clarity you notice some trifle on the side ... and (all this simultaneously) the convergence is joined by a third thought—the memory of a sunny evening at a Russian small railway station .... (163; 344)

So, if we dare compare this idea to how we could perceive a window, the first level—see through a man clearly as if he was made of glass—parallels with how we see the outside view through the window; the second level—to notice particular details—might correspond to noticing usually neglected details on the windowpane itself; the third level—memory—may be equal to perceiving the reflection (synonymous with "memory") in the window.

The following window scene can also be said "multiplied," yet in a slightly different way: "A train stretched over the viaduct: the yawn begun by a woman in the lighted window of the first car was completed by another woman—in the last one" (325; 500). Here again in Nabokov's work a moment of illusionist fantasy is rendered by train windows. Unlike the majority of train window episodes, however, in this case the view is a remote one from the outside looking in, and by Fyodor's optical magic, a window and a woman in it (or, to borrow Nabokov's intonation elsewhere, a window and its woman) is assimilated into another window and its woman. This is an example of Fyodor's "flexibility of switching modes of perception independent of watched objects."[30] This tendency of Fyodor might be a cause of the confusing arrangement of parks and squares in the novel, the question to be taken up in the next chapter of this dissertation.

---

[30] Berdjis, *Imagery*, 253.

−73−

Reading Nabokov's Framed Landscape

Those windows mentioned above are all "real" ones that Fyodor really sees. More significant windows, however, appear as imagined ones. We will examine two such windows here. One appears while the narrator contemplates "longing for one's homeland:"

> Ought one not to reject any longing for one's homeland, for any homeland besides that which is with me, within me, which is stuck like the silver sand of the sea to the skin of my soles, lives in my eyes, my blood, gives depth and distance to the background of life's every hope? Some day, interrupting my writing, I will look through the window and see a Russian autumn. (175; 356)

This is not exclusively the "narrator's" thought but that of both the narrator and Fyodor, for this is a part of a paragraph that begins with the remark "Suddenly he felt a bitter pang," thus in a third-person voice, and then goes on to tell Fyodor's opinion on and feeling toward Russia, and in this process the narrator gradually shifts his voice from third-person to first-person via a momentary usage of the rather neutral "one" (this is, in this narrator's case, a typical way of changing modes of narrative). Therefore, there is considerable ambiguity concerning who exactly is imagining this window. Alternatively, it may be both (for, they could be regarded as the same person in the end), so this window reflects both Fyodor the character's and that of the narrator's. The narrator's room and Fyodor's room coincide here for a moment, by means of one imagined window. Maybe the narrator looks through his own window now, but we cannot know what he could see: this is natural because "a Russian autumn" is only in his eye, thus inaccessible and invisible to others. Here we remember Fyodor's remark "my eyes are, in the long run, made of the same stuff as the grayness, the clarity, the dampness of those sites" (25; 211) and an already quoted comment on this by Berdjis "the beholder and what he beholds merge into one." The narrator's eye, already merged with what he had once consumed with his eye, could reproduce and project it on any window, as if his eye contained in it picture films to be projected on a linen screen by a magic-

-74-

Chapter II Nabokov through Windowpanes

lantern.[31] Fyodor, as the narrator somewhat predicted, in his already dark room looks through the window immediately after this passage, and sees the darkening sky above "the blackened outlines of the houses beyond the yard, where the windows were already alight" (175-76; 356). The narrator continues:

> . . . the sky had an ultramarine shade and in the black wires between black chimneys there shone a star—which, like any star, could only properly be seen by switching one's vision, so that all the rest moved away out of focus. He propped his cheek on his fist and sat there at the table, looking through the window. (176; 356)

The window does not seem to yield anything special, but this star remains in his memory, reflects its gleam in his verse on the next page as "yonder star above the Volga glows," (177; 357) and, perhaps, reappears at the very end of the book: "And one day we shall recall all this—the lindens, and the shadows on the wall, and a poodle's unclipped claws tapping over the flagstones of the night. And the star, the star" (366; 541). The star here may be regarded as what Fyodor and Zina could see at that moment in the sky, not directly referring to the star on page 176; however, both scenes being set in summer, it is highly possible that they are really an identical star. Moreover, by being framed in his window and focused by Fyodor's eye, the former star cannot easily fade away in our memory, so that the short, yet suggestive and mysterious phrase "And the star, the star" brings that star back to us, letting us recognize it.

Now, finally, we can deal with the other "imagined" window. In Chapter 5, the narrator suddenly (and almost imperceptibly) starts to speak in the voice of the dying Alexander Yakovlevich Chernyshevski, Fyodor's friend, and in this monologue he topographically describes the relation-

---

[31] Chapter 8 of *Speak, Memory* shows Nabokov's love for a magic-lantern show. Nabokov's memory is often termed a "photographic memory," but here in this context, the image of a magic-lantern is more apt.

−75−

Reading Nabokov's Framed Landscape

ship between this world and hereafter: "...we are not going anywhere, we are sitting at home. The other world surrounds us always and is not at all at the end of some pilgrimage. In our earthly house, windows are replaced by mirrors; the door, until a given time, is closed" (310; 484). As he (it does not really matter whether "he" is Chernyshevski or the narrator) himself admits, all this is "only symbols" and should not be taken seriously, nor should be considered as Nabokov's perception of hereafter. In his last moment of lucidity, Chernyshevski says, "What nonsense. Of course there is nothing afterwards," listening to the "tickling and drumming outside the window," and then repeats, "There is nothing. It is as clear as the fact that it is raining." However, the fact is that "outside the spring sun was playing on the roof tiles, the sky was dreamy and cloudless, the tenant upstairs was watering the flowers on the edge of her balcony..." (312; 487). This scene is one that has been thoroughly discussed by critics, for its featuring of Nabokov's favored pattern of a belief followed immediately by a refutation. The deceptive window in Chernyshevski's room renders his idea about the topography of other world unreliable.

We have examined a variety of windows playing their own multiple roles in the novel, and now may acknowledge them as being a motif particularly favored by Nabokov. However, when one tries to talk about "hereafter" through the metaphor of the window, it suddenly becomes quite doubtful, fragile, even useless. It is because death is beyond imagination, beyond any metaphor. After the discussion about the white pencil, Fyodor says, "It's a pity one can't imagine what one can't compare to anything." This novel is full of comparisons and metaphors, which is of course quite typical in Nabokov's world, for "his language is a continual attempt to find fresh metaphors, original similes, to unite objects that appear to be totally unlike."[32] However, "hereafter" seems not to allow any metaphor, any description. "I know more than I can express in words," once answered Nabokov to his interviewer, "and the little I can express would not have been expressed, had I not known more" (SO 45). The landscape of "hereaf-

−76−

Chapter II Nabokov through Windowpanes

ter" is in this unexpressed region, for which no writing instrument is useful, except for one: the white pencil. With this instrument, as we saw, he can produce anything he imagines, even that which he cannot express with words.

---

[32] Stegner, Page. *Escape into Aesthetics: The Art of Vladimir Nabokov.* New York: The Dial Press, 1966, 55.

Chapter III
Mapping out Fyodor's Berlin

1. The Square Motif

Kinbote, a great lover of window views, confesses his attachment to a particular window that always provides him with "a first-rate entertainment," and from which he peeps into "the Shades' living-room window" (*PF* 23), thus seeing his favorite poet John Shade as a framed picture (in the same way that Humbert sometimes sees Lolita as a painted picture). His description of the view from a window initially maps out the relation of Shade's house to Kinbote's (*PF* 87) before evolving into a verbal map of the wider city, starting from his street (Dulwich Road) to the university where they teach, and also to the airport.[1] His preference for maps can be observed also in "a rather handsomely drawn plan of the chambers, terraces, bastions and pleasure grounds of the Onhava Palace" (*PF* 106). Kinbote, believing that this "careful picture in colored inks" of the king's (or Kinbote's) palace is now in the hand of Mrs Shade, in vain writes to her in the hope of getting it back. Kinbote's hanker for the plan is inexplicably strong, especially because "these excruciating headaches now make impossible the mnemonic effort and eye strain that the drawing of another such plan would demand" (*PF* 107). For him the plan is as precious as "crown

---

[1] Kinbote even likens his own description to a landscape, explaining that "the dull pain of distance is rendered through an effect of style" and "a topographical idea finds its verbal expression in a series of foreshortened sentences" (*PF* 92).

Chapter III Mapping out Fyodor's Berlin

jewels," whose whereabouts are a chief puzzle in this novel, and, as he cannot find the crown jewels, the plan also remains unattainable. Unlike Nabokov, Kinbote cannot reproduce from memory a map of the place where he used to live (or so he believes at least), and the lost map has almost the same value as the place itself.

Nabokov, as a commentator to Pushkin's *Eugene Onegin*, shows the same passion towards mapping as Kinbote, the annotator of Shade's long poem. There is a rich note concerning "bodies of waters" mentioned in *Onegin*, in which Nabokov tries to clarify the arrangement of those rivers, brooks and streamlets in the topography of this verse-novel; he finds that "the streamlets ... of Onegin's brook reach Krasnogorie and Lenski's grave" and "fall into a river," which "runs through the Larins' estate," and that "the Larins' river is supplemented ... by a brook or brooks," which "undergoes strange transformations" in Tatiana's dream; finally he suspects that "the same waters that connect the three country places are those which (now frozen) pertain to the mill ... near which Lenski is dispatched in his duel with Onegin" (*EO* II 200-03). His searching exploration into the novel's topography based on the water arrangement reveals the fact that he puts a lot of care into mapping when reading a book.[2]

Nabokov states that "instructors should prepare maps of Dublin with Bloom's and Stephen's intertwining itineraries clearly traced," and that "[w]ithout a visual perception of the larch labyrinth in *Mansfield Park* that novel loses some of its stereographic charm" (*SO* 157). Following his instruction, the reader should try to make a map of his works; in this chapter we will explore his most labyrinthine city—Fyodor's Berlin in *The Gift*, imitating Nabokov's way of producing a map through such a key motif as

---

[2] Tammi, in his argument about the peculiarities that the topography of Nabokov's St. Petersburg show, points out: "There is a tradition of treating the topographical details occurring in Russian literature with some seriousness" (Tammi, Pekka. *Russian Subtexts in Nabokov's Fiction: Four essays.* Tampere: Tampere UP, 1999. 71).

−79−

Reading Nabokov's Framed Landscape

that of a river: the motif we use here is "square."

First of all it is worth pointing out the unreliable and erroneous nature of Fyodor's topography: he "always had bad marks in geography" (107; 290), and admits there are "many topographical errors" (137; 320) in his references to the regions his father was supposed to visit. The narrator, if we dare to recognize him as Fyodor in future, therefore seems to construct his own version of Berlin, which is crowded with mysterious, labyrinthine streets, making the reader lose his way. Berlin in this novel does not seem stable; it keeps changing, always under construction. We will examine the way the narrator describes the streets and discuss the meaning of this transformation from the real, existing Berlin to a changeable, fairy-tale city. What confuses the city's order is, as mentioned above, squares and public gardens. Though there are more than ten references to squares and public gardens in this book, we seem to fail to identify exactly how many squares and public gardens there are: some of them resemble each other to such a degree, differing only in slight details that we struggle to discern which square is which. In the Russian version the word "*skver*" corresponds both to the "square" and the "public garden," while the original Russian for the English "square" has always at least two possibilities— "*skver*" and "*proshad*.'" The identity of squares seems more uncertain in the Russian version because Russian has no article, making it difficult for the reader to judge if this or that park is one already mentioned before or not. However, even in the English version, with all its articles, they remain still as vague as in the Russian original.

The first square in the book, appearing on Fyodor's way to the Chernyshevski where a literary soiree is due to be held, is described in the following manner: "He . . . quickly finished them [piroshki] off on a damp bench in a small public garden ["*skver*"]" (30; 216). Keeping this in mind, let us read the following passage relating Fyodor's way back from the Chernyshevski in the same evening:

Here at last is the square ["*skver*"] where we dined and the tall brick

– 80 –

Chapter III Mapping out Fyodor's Berlin

church and the still quite transparent poplar, resembling the nervous
system of a giant; here, also, is the public toilet, reminiscent of Baba
Yaga's gingerbread cottage. In the gloom of the small public garden
["*skver*"] crossed obliquely by the faint light of a streetlamp, the
beautiful girl . . . was sitting on a cinder-gray bench, but when he
got closer he saw that only the bent shadow of the poplar trunk was
sitting there. (53; 239)

The passage above has always been a problematic point of discussion, chal-
lenging the reader to define who the "we" refers to. It is also this very ambiguous "we" that further confuses the geography of this novel. Most critics, including Connolly[3], identify the "we" as the character Fyodor and his
lover, Zina, and identify the square here as "a treeless public garden
["*skver*"]" where they dine toward the end of the book (362; 537). However, as Dolinin observes, the two squares have nothing in common, and so
may well be considered as two completely different squares; in that case,
"the square we dined" signifies the first public garden where Fyodor dines
off those piroshki alone, and the "we" means Fyodor the character and Fyodor the narrator.[4] It may not be important to determine which is the right
interpretation: it is presumable that Nabokov intended this phrase to be
ambiguous, leaving the reader at least two possible answers.

The problem of identifying those three squares is extended further to
the last square in the novel. The following line can be seen at the end of
the book, after another problematic passage containing the ambiguous
"we": "And here is the square and the dark church with the yellow light of
its clock" (366; 541). We feel relieved to locate at last the origin of the
sound of a chime mentioned elsewhere: "In the distance a large clock
(whose position he was always promising himself to define, but always for-

---

[3] Connolly, *Nabokov's Early Fiction*, 217.
[4] Dolinin, Alexander. "*The Gift*," in *Garland Companion to Vladimir Nabokov*. Ed. Vladimir E. Alexandrov. New York: Garland, 1995. 164-65

got, the more so since it was never audible under the layer of daytime sounds) slowly chimed nine o'clock" (176; 356). This church also seems familiar to us, if we remember the description of the square on page 53: "Here at last is the square where we dined and the tall brick church." At the same time, however, this last square, without any detail, is actually the most undetermined and abstract of all, making the reader feel themself getting lost. No matter what the reality is, we are still inclined to identify the square on page 53 with the one at the last page, especially because the problematic "we" links these two scenes.

In the former square (on page 53), besides the church there are "the still quite transparent poplar," "the public toilet, reminiscent of Baba Yaga's gingerbread cottage," and "the small public garden." We need to remember those details of the square in one spring evening.

About six pages later Fyodor visits "the square" ["*skver*"] in which garden there is "a young chestnut tree" and "[t]he lilacs" (59; 245). There is also "the church," "the locust tree," and "the rose beds around the statue of a bronze runner" (60; 245). The narrator then depicts Fyodor bathing in the June sun on "an indigo bench in the public garden ["*skver*"]" (60; 245). Is this the same square as the previous one? Every detail looks new, giving the impression that this square is a different one from any of those described before. At the same time one cannot deny the possibility that the square in question might be identified as the second square, "the square where we dined."

What is worth noting here is the presence of a bench in each of the first three squares. As we will clarify in the next section of this chapter, a bench is a special, favored device in Nabokov's works. So, let us now go back to the first square to take a close look at the "damp bench" where Fyodor dines in the evening. The "damp" in the English version here only means the dampness from the rain (for it has been raining), while the Russian equivalent "*syraya*" (the feminine of "*syroi*"), besides the ordinary meanings such as "damp" "raw," signifies "incomplete" or "lacking polish"

−82−

Chapter III Mapping out Fyodor's Berlin

when used to qualify a literary work. We could dare imagine here a bench that has been just painted, thus being still wet: a fresh but still unpolished bench at the beginning of the book could foreshadow the nature of the city itself (and also this book)—always under construction, changeable and slippery.

When we return to the second park in the night ("the square where we dined"), we also encounter "a cinder-gray bench," while in the third square where Fyodor bathes in the sun has "an indigo bench." Every one of the three differently-colored benches mentioned above appears with an indefinite article, and therefore could be regarded as a different bench; at the same time they could be seen as one identical bench, for the three scenes are set respectively at about sunset, at night, and in the daytime, making it possible to render varied tinges and atmosphere to the bench in the same square. We can easily accept the possibility of change of color and shape that a given place undergoes over the course of time, all the more because in the night streets Fyodor (and Fyodor the narrator) is always aware of something mysterious that he cannot find in the daytime.

Besides the possibility of hourly transformation of color and shape, a lot of other types of transformation can be observed in the setting of this novel, from the accumulation of which the reader gets lost still further.[5] To see a curious example, let us go back again to "the square we dined." There we find "the public toilet, reminiscent of Baba Yaga's gingerbread cottage." We must keep in mind that Baba Yaga, a popular hag in Russian folklore, is referred to as only a part of simile here. Now, on page 63, it is autumn and here we come across a scene that is too curious to believe: "Carrying a broom, the little old woman in a clean apron, with a small sharp face and disproportionately large feet, came out of her gingerbread

---

[5] Berdjis, in chapter 2 ("Metamorphoses") of his work, shows in full detail the "images according to the transition they achieve between two different realms" (*Imagery in Vladimir Nabokov's last Russian Novel*, 18).

−83−

cottage with its candy windows" (63; 249). A reader who remembers that public toilet must become exquisitely confused, not knowing how to interpret this phenomenon: this gingerbread cottage seems most likely to be identical with "the public toilet" in the first square, but if it is so, did the toilet metamorphose into the real cottage of Baba Yaga? Then we have to conclude that this old woman who strikingly resembles Baba Yaga has magically entered Fyodor's real world from the realm of simile.[6] This enigmatic description of Baba Yaga with her cottage works to produce a vague, unstable, mysterious air in Fyodor's Berlin. If we deny the possibility of this metamorphosis, ignoring a link between the two places above, the book's charm and potential may considerably be reduced.

We will study another pair of squares, one of which, though, is not actually a square: "It was a windy and shabby crossroads, not quite grown to the rank of a square ["*proshad*"] although there was a church, and a public garden ["*skver*"], and a corner pharmacy, and a public convenience with thujas around it . . ." (161; 342). Also we should remember that behind the garden there is "an abandoned soccer field" (162; 343).

If one memorizes them, one will be able to find a striking resemblance between the crossroad above and the square ["*proshad*"] which appears at the scene of Chernyshevski's cremation. One of the marks that link them is "a football field" (313; 488). The other marker is in the following line: "He found himself by the bronze boxers; in the flower beds around them rippled pale, black-blotched pansies (somewhat similar facially to Charlie Chaplin) . . ." (314; 489). A figure of Chaplin appears near the crossroad above, thus making us inclined to connect the two places: "Over the entrance to a cinema a black giant cut out of cardboard had been erected, with turned-out feet, the blotch of a mustache on his white face beneath a

---

[6] Nabokov notes a curious tendency of "the comparison-generated character" to "join the life of the book" in Gogol's *The Dead Soul* (*Lectures on Russian Literature*, 22). Nabokov seems to apply Gogol's method in a further developed form here.

Chapter III Mapping out Fyodor's Berlin

bowler hat, and a bent cane in his hand" (162; 343). It may be assumed
that the crossroad above is metamorphosed, or grew up, to the square: a
"shabby crossroad" after all has "grown to the rank of a square." The image
of growth in the square in question is clearly reflected also in such phrases
as "the green cupolas of a white Pskovan-type church, which had recently
grown up out of the corner house" and "two badly wrought bronze boxers,
also recently erected" (313; 488). It might be a variation of the growth
theme and at the same time it looks like magic, or a sudden metamorphosis of the place.

On another occasion magic is secretly performed immediately before
Fyodor reaches "the square where we dined": ". . . with a magic tinkling, by
the light of crimson lanterns, dim beings ["*nevidimki*"] were repairing the
pavement at the corner of the square ["*proshad*"]. . ." (52; 238). The Russian "*nevidimki*" is, primarily, the general term in fairytales for both beings
and inanimate beings endowed with a gift of making themselves invisible.
The English equivalent "dim beings" doesn't sound as mysterious as the
Russian, but still retains some of its original magic tone. The magic air of
the corner of the square will reveal itself more distinctly, when superimposed on a street visited in Fyodor's "dream" where he reunites with his
dead father (a dream in quotation marks, for the scene is written as real as
any other part, with no indication that this is a dream). Here in the dream
city Fyodor and the reader seem to revisit that same, dreamlike corner of
the square, for we find: "Some night workers had wrecked the pavement at
the corner" (352; 528). The "dim beings" become now the "night workers"
and still continue to work on this corner. It is worth noting that while the
pavement is being repaired at the beginning of the novel, it is now
"wrecked" toward the end of the novel, which seems slightly preposterous,
but at the same time implies the theme of endless interchange of construction and destruction in this book. What really matters here is the fact that
the "real" street now seems as dreamlike as the street in dream, giving us
the impression that Fyodor's real world and the realm of dream are con-

− 85 −

nected by some hidden streets, thus without any boundary between them—this also confuses and diversifies the map of Fyodor's Berlin.

We are not able to locate correctly these squares above: one square seems to resemble another, though at the same time they look totally different, discouraging the reader from drawing a map of Berlin in Fyodor's version. One of the hints explaining the labyrinthine structure of his Berlin might be found in the following passage: "Waiting for her [Zina's] arrival. She was always late—and always came by another road than he. Thus it transpired that even Berlin could be mysterious" (176; 357). It is clear that the narrator is using "mysterious" as a desirable word, as the opposite image of prosaic plainness that Fyodor more commonly associates with Berlin. The city's mystery is intensified by the following passage that shows how Zina appears "out of darkness":

> At first her ankles would catch the light: she moved them close together as if she walked along a slender rope. Her summer dress was short, of night's own color, the color of the streetlights and the shadows, of tree trunks and of shining pavement—paler than her bare arms and darker than her face. (177; 357)

Here Zina is described with the image of mimesis and looks almost transparent. Here, as Zina comes by another road than he, unexpected streets seem to be hiding everywhere; or, it is as if new roads continued to be paved endlessly by following the wake of the character's footsteps, producing the impression of an inchoate city. Most interestingly, the whole passage above gives us quite a contrary impression at the same time, that is, Zina seems to emerge from the night street. We will discuss the matter more fully in the next chapter.

In the mysterious and labyrinthine world that comprises Fyodor's Berlin it is possible that sometimes one single thing appears to be two different objects, and at other times vice versa; an object which is imperceptible in the daytime grows visible at night, as in the case of "some strange arcades" (327; 502); the color of a bench shifts from cinder-gray in the

– 86 –

Chapter III Mapping out Fyodor's Berlin

moonlight to indigo in the sun; and the number of squares is infinite. His intricate Berlin looks like a kaleidoscope, with identical motifs radiating from the center: the almost identical (yet quite different) squares with their changeability and rich details correspond to colorful motifs harmoniously distributed around the center, and those details, given successive shakes, are endlessly transfigured by the author's (Fyodor the author's) agile, hypnotizing hand. In doing so, Fyodor the author tries to discover mystery, magic and charm in the "real" Berlin, which the other Fyodor finds so prosaic and vulgar.

Although every street and every square seem to somehow head for Grunewalt where Fyodor experiences a kind of epiphany towards the end of the novel, the reader still cannot make out the arrangement of and the relationships between each street and square. One of the reasons for the disrupted topography may be derived from the following remark on Fyodor's incapability to remember the exact place, in his pseudo-review of *Poem*: "... already I am beginning to forget relationships and connections between objects that still thrive in my memory ..." (18; 205). This passing remark should not be forgotten, for this is one of the factors that work to show the contrast between Fyodor and Chernyshevski. Fyodor, in his biography of this historical figure, refers to the plans of apartments drawn by Chernyshevki in his letters: "The exact definition of the relations between objects always fascinated him and therefore he loved plans, columns of figures and visual representations of things ..." (218; 397). For Chernyshevski the entire picture of a certain place and how each object inside is connected are important. Fyodor, on the other hand, forgetful of connections between things, seems almost unconcerned about how this square is related to that. His map, therefore, lacks paths that connect each topographical detail, making the impression that each square or street is complete in itself, existing independently without any relation to any other place; at the same time, however, they all somehow look alike, easily commingled and always overlapping with each other. This overlapping nature can be found

−87−

not only in the perception of space but also in that of time in this novel. Past, present and future are not arranged in a sequential fashion, but coexist simultaneously, easily allowing Fyodor to slip into a different time. This fractal nature of Fyodor's Berlin somewhat reminds us of "the secret of the world" related by Busch, a writer who helped Fyodor publish his biography of Chernyshevski: "The whole is equal to the smallest part of the whole, the sum of the parts is equal to one part of the sum" (210; 390). As the whole city is complete in itself, its smallest parts—squares and streets that mimic each other and even "the whole" city—similarly form its own complete universe. What we can draw from the descriptions of the streets and square is not a map of the entire city but a series of highly detailed, independent parts. Most importantly, it seems that one cannot revisit the same square again: although the narrator says "Here at last the square where we dined," we cannot still completely be sure about the identity of those two squares. We can never see a given public garden twice: every garden seems to possess a temporary existence, unable to be revisited. The squares therefore may function as a symbol of an irretrievable place and time.

Lastly, let us take a closer examination of the relationship of the writer to the city. We may recall that "world of cold water" that "caused his head to ache" (158; 338) at the bathroom. It reminds us of Fyodor's remark, in his last letter to his mother, that Berlin (Germany) is "the terribly cold world around me" and is "oppressive as a headache" (350; 525). It is in the lake, in his father's embrace, and in Zina's presence that the coldness disappears. However, for some reason, we do not feel this coldness of Berlin's in Fyodor the author's narrative and realize a certain gap between Fyodor the character's sentiment toward Berlin and Fyodor the author's tone of describing the city. Consultation of Fyodor's letter, in which he confesses "I'd abandon tomorrow this country, oppressive as a headache—where everything is alien and repulsive to me" (350; 525) enables us to know Fyodor's candid feelings towards this country. However, except for this letter, such a strong repulsion and hatred toward the country are hardly perceptible

Chapter III Mapping out Fyodor's Berlin

(though it is true there are some remarks on the vulgarity of Berliners) throughout the novel. In other words, the strong repulsion and alienation openly expressed in Fyodor's letter are to a great extent alleviated in Fyodor the author's narration. It is conceivable that this alleviation or control over Fyodor the character's feeling is a reflection of the writer's generosity and even gratitude toward Berlin—the city that gave Fyodor "wonderful solitude" and his warm "inner habitus" (350; 525). The narrator, instead of expressing clearly the negative side of Berlin, tries to discover and shed light on (and perhaps invent) the mysterious, beautiful side of the city.

Finally, Fyodor the author prepares an unusual gift (for the reader and Fyodor): the last evening of this book, with its beautiful, rich imagery, becomes a gift itself in an enormous box. This idea is not so groundless if we remember the following remark: "He remembered with incredible vividness, as if he had preserved that sunny day in a velvet case, his father's last return, in July 1912" (125; 308-9). This day is described as a gift in a velvet case, and the same applies to the evening of June 29, 1929.[7] We have a highly expressive passage for this image: "'Look,' he said. 'What a beauty!' A brooch with three rubies was gliding over the dark velvet . ." (362; 537). The narrator continues the image of jewels in a velvet case, explaining that Fyodor's happiness is "also expressed" by "such things as the velvetiness of the air, three emerald lime leaves that had got into the lamplight" (363; 538). The image of Fyodor and Zina in this gift box with the velvet lining together with those rubies and emeralds is far from that repulsive Berlin, the world of cold water: "Berlin" here is totally reconstructed into a warm, otherworldly city by our author.

Setting Grunewald at the center, the author Fyodor distributes un-

---

[7] The question of the book's terminal year is hard to solve: most critics define it as 1929, following the chronology Nabokov himself suggested, and there is also an argument, "on the basis of (somewhat arguable) 'internal evidence,' that the correct terminal year should rather be 1928." (*Russian Subtext* 98).

– 89 –

counted, mirror-like squares around it. Among the intricate, kaleidoscopic pattern of streets which after all lead to the center, Fyodor can accidentally find the secret paths to another "reality"—to the paradise of the past, to the dreamland Berlin where son and father reunite, and to the lyrical evening world with Zina. Fyodor the author, by constructing the city as a labyrinth that enables Fyodor the character to stray into the places where he can meet his dearest people, succeeds in softening Fyodor's alienation and repulsion, and at the same time tries to speak about Berlin generously, with a thankful heart. The totally reformed topography of the city makes any journey possible.

2. The Bench Motifs

What we repeatedly came across while recreating the map of Fyodor's Berlin was a bench. Indeed Nabokov's works abound with scenes that feature a bench, and once we realize their constant presence, they generously begin to show us how beautifully they hide underneath valuable keys to read Nabokov's books; they are not just randomly scattered but are selectively, intentionally placed in necessary points, and when we look closely around those scenes, we may detect there some features highly characteristic of Nabokov's fiction. Several such scenes in *The Gift* reveal some stylistic technique that may give us a key to the novel's complex narration. Focusing mainly on this novel, we will attempt to recognize long abandoned "bench" as a special motif of Nabokov's fiction.

The transparent drawing on the child Nabokov's pillow from which we started our research already contained a bench: we remember well how he fondly followed with his forefinger the "carved back of a bench." As an object forming his cherished early scenery, this bench must be indispensable. Another "carved back of a bench" appears at the beginning of Chapter 6 (entitled "Butterflies") of *Speak, Memory*. To our surprise, the opening of this chapter is a rare spot where three themes of our main concern

Chapter III Mapping out Fyodor's Berlin

delightfully commingle together: the window theme, the motif of picture, and the bench motif.[8] Nabokov begins by telling us that his first glance upon awakening on a summer morning was "for the chink between the white inner shutters" (*SM* 94), and that if "it disclosed a watery pallor, one had better not open them at all, and so be spared the sight of a sullen day sitting for its picture in a puddle." Nabokov the verbal painter, however, cannot help producing a picture himself, based on an image reflected in an imaginary puddle: "How resentfully one would deduce, from a line of dull light, the leaden sky, the sodden sand, the gruel-like mess of broken brown blossoms under the lilacs—and that flat, fallow leaf (the first casualty of the season) pasted upon a wet garden bench!" (*SM* 94). Next he shows how he "made haste to have the window yield its treasure" when the chink "was a long glint of dewy brilliancy." For the child Nabokov, "a rectangle of framed sunlight," that is, the window brimmed with sunlight, in the morning, means nothing but promise of butterflies. He tells us "the original event" in the following manner:

> On the honeysuckle, overhanging the carved back of a bench just opposite the main entrance, my guiding angel (whose wings, except for the absence of a Florentine limbus, resemble those of Fra Angelico's Gabriel) pointed out to me a rare visitor, a splendid, pale-yellow creature with black blotches, blue crenels, and a cinnabar eyespot above each chrome-rimmed black tail. (*SM* 94)

The picture of the bench and the butterfly here forms a singular contrast to that imagined picture of the wet bench: it seems that the "fallow leaf," the "casualty," is resurrected in the form of this splendid butterfly in an inspiriting sunlight. The imagined bench and the real bench, therefore, collaborate in a conjuring trick of producing a butterfly from a dead leaf.

---

[8] The chapter also offers us a beautiful little scene with a window where the boy himself is likened to a butterfly: "Breakfastless, with hysterical haste, I gathered my net, pill boxes, killing jar, and *escaped through the window* [italic added]" (*SM* 100).

Reading Nabokov's Framed Landscape

A bench first appears in *The Gift* not as a real one but as one that is re-membered, which might be modeled from the bench above. In the pseu-do-review of his book of poetry, the reviewer (Fyodor) explains how Fyo-dor "reconstructed everything," "as a returning traveler sees in an orphan's eyes not only the smile of its mother, whom he had known in his youth, but also an avenue ending in a burst of yellow light and that auburn leaf on the bench, and everything, everything" (10; 197). This line not only recalls the bench in Nabokov's memoir shown above but also naturally echoes what the 5-year-old Nabokov did with his memory, imagination and his forefinger.

The concluding section of the butterfly chapter of *Speak, Memory* again contains benches, this time as "Turgenevian benches" (*SM* 107). Note in the Library of America version of this memoir says: "From Turgenev's having his characters encounter one another in such settings so often in his fiction." [9] In one aspect, some benches appearing in Nabokov's works are inevitably Turgenevian, for an author cannot completely free from an influence past writers of his own country have (especially so, for Russian literature has this long tradition of using a bench as a convenient setting). [10] His benches, therefore, must be in the long continuing line of Russian pre-dilection for benches, but at the same time are endowed with a unique, new characteristic by Nabokov.

The first major bench in the novel is, as already examined previously, "a damp bench in a small public garden" (30; 216) on which he dines off piro-shki. The "damp bench" here could be traced back to the "damp garden bench" which Fyodor quotes from Goncharov, not Turgenev, in a discus-

---

[9] Nabokov, Vladimir. *Novels and Memoirs. 1941-1951*. New York: Library of America, 1996. 702.

[10] Again in his notes to *Eugene Onegin*, for example, Nabokov comments: "Pushkin's description of Tatiana's dash from dining room to park bench gives the reader an idea of the ground" (*EO* II 406), and starts to follow her path carefully, in a manner already familiar to us.

Chapter III Mapping out Fyodor's Berlin

sion on Russian literature with Koncheyev. Fyodor, however, refers to Goncharov's bench here as a representative of things that he teases and finds tasteless in Russian literature. This fact tells us that *The Gift* cannot exist without Russian works of the past, including those which the protagonist rates low. An ordinary bench that the narrator (or the author) inherited from Goncharov, though, develops into a special device through the progress of the novel. We will study four significant scenes where a bench provides a special setting for the narrative.

A Bench in the Sun—Shifting Voices

A bench in a square is a recurrent setting in Nabokov's works. We will again visit a sunny square mentioned in the previous section and subject it to a closer study. It is important to keep it in mind that the passage in question relates a scene that could be seen repeatedly through June and July.

> Fyodor, in his shirt-sleeves and with sneakers on his sockless feet, would spend the greater part of the day on an indigo bench in the public garden, a book in his long tanned fingers; and when the sun beat down too hard, he would lean his head on the hot back of the bench and shut his eyes for long periods ... but now the scarlet darkened under a passing cloud, and lifting his sweaty neck, he would open his eyes and once again see the park, the lawn with its marguerites, the freshly watered gravel, the little girl playing hopscotch with herself, the pram with the baby consisting of two eyes and a pink rattle .... (60; 245)

The insistent use of the "would" every time reminds the reader that this is a habitual, repeated scene, and does not limit itself to one specific day. Still, each minute detail does create the impression that this should be a description of one specific moment, impossible to be repeated. This ambiguity of time created from the use of the "would" is highly characteristic of

– 93 –

Reading Nabokov's Framed Landscape

Nabokov's narrative.[11]

The narration relating a habitual, repeated action in the past is often accompanied by the problem of shifting voices. Immediately before the scene above where Fyodor is invited to the square the narrator (Fyodor the narrator) talks about the painter Romanov in the first person, using Fyodor the character's voice, but after the following line: "That sun was already inviting me into the square" (59; 245) the narrator stops using the first person pronoun and shifts to the third person narration, and to the description of a habitual scene of the past.[12] After the scene in the square the narrator continues to present Fyodor's work as a private teacher of English ("he would go to give lesson") and how he enters the newspaper office to bring his composed poems as repeated actions, using mostly the "would." The whole description here provides the funny impression that Fyodor the character becomes gradually invisible, especially so in the long passage describing the interior of the newspaper office, composed with the sentences lacking both the word "Fyodor" and the "he," where the narrator, almost forgetting the presence of Fyodor there, keeps describing the details not through Fyodor's eye but through his own perception. In the following part, for instance, the narrator uses the subject "one," which sounds almost impersonal: "The telephone jangled . . . 'Why, do we owe you money? Nothing of the kind, the secretary would say.' When the door to the room on the right opened, one could hear the juicily dictating voice of Getz, or Stupishin clearing his throat . . ." (61; 246). In the Russian original this is expressed with a sentence of indefinite person. In this way the first person narrative in which the character Fyodor's existence in a particular time can

---

[11] In the Russian original Nabokov is using past imperfective, which expresses the process of action in the past or a repeated action, and could be rendered by the use of the English "would."

[12] The Russian version here lacks a corresponding word for "me," hence the first person narrative is supposed to be imperceptibly finished somewhere earlier.

Chapter III Mapping out Fyodor's Berlin

be perceived shifts to the third person narrative, and finally to the narrative where any "person" seems not to be present.

The pivotal point which calls the reader's attention to Fyodor the character's body and consciousness in this shifting process is the bench scene quoted above, which is marked by the alternating emergence of the sun and Fyodor's eyes: his eyes close when the sun which is described through the metaphor of an eye (cf. "the journey of the blinded, breathing, radiant disk through the cloud") is hidden behind the clouds and vice versa. Connolly suggests that in the Grunewald scene the sun "which begins to transform (or "translate") the narrating entity into itself may be an emblem of a higher authorial consciousness—that which is responsible for creating the character Fyodor."[13] The early sign of the sun's role, therefore, could be already perceived here in the bench scene. The alternating opening and closing of Fyodor's and the sun's eyes seems to allude to the way the first-person narrative and the third-person narrative alternate in a series of passages that center around the bench scene: the first person narrative in Fyodor the character's voice corresponds to the moment where Fyodor's eye is open, while the moment when the sunlight becomes strong, opening its eye and then shutting Fyodor's eye almost coincides with the shift into the third-person narration.[14] The complex shifts of the narrative perspective is what we cannot ignore when discussing the novel; this seemingly ordinary bench scene should be observed more closely as a critical point in terms of the narrative style.

---

[13] Connolly, *Early Fiction*, 212.

[14] We may be expected to deal with the expression "shut his eyes" more carefully, since Nabokov originally used the verb "*jmuritza*," which signifies the act of half-opening or squinting one's eyes. The corresponding Russian expression for "to shut (close) eyes" should be "*zakryt' glaza*." To examine fully a difference between the completely closed eyes in the English version and the half-closed ones in the original would require another paper.

– 95 –

Dialogue on a Bench

Next we are going to focus on the image of a couple in conversation on a bench. We have two main samples, one of which is the imaginary conversation in Grunewald between Fyodor and a poet Koncheyev. Fyodor finds a "young man in a black suit" sitting on a bench beneath an oak tree, and the narrator, first defining the young man as Koncheyev, starts to relate their longish conversation through the third-person (337-38; 512). At the end of the record of the dialogue, however, he confesses the man was only a German who resembles Koncheyev, and immediately after this abruptly shifts to the first-person voice: "Imagination again—but what a pity! I had even thought up a dead mother for him in order to trap truth. . ." (343; 518). Of particular interest here is the ambiguous identity of the first-person pronoun "I" who "imagined" this conversation. Connolly acknowledges Fyodor's artistic maturity in the way the whole Grunewald scene, particularly in the invented conversation with Koncheyev, is described, pointing out that compared to a corresponding dialogue in Chapter 1 the description here "is not marred by lapses in the illusion that these are two separate entities," indicating "the clarity of the separation" between "the creative consciousness (self)" and "the object of creative perception (other)." [15] The first-person narrator becomes gradually separated also from the character Fyodor through the novel, hence the "I" who invented the conversation with the poet, saying "Imagination again," could be regarded not as Fyodor the character there in the past but as the present narrator, who is writing this now, remote from the young character Fyodor. We notice, therefore, a slight difference between the "I"-narrator immediately before the first bench scene (where a dialogue between Fyodor and the sun is illustrated) discussed earlier and that in the present passage above. It can be said that the narrator uses benches as a place where he could be highly imaginative

---

[15] Connolly, *Early Fiction*, 209.

Chapter III Mapping out Fyodor's Berlin

and shows the readers an illusion, and also where he (or the author) tries to attract the readers' attention to the system of the narrative and a moderate change, development, of the narrator's artifice.

The other pivotal scene of a bench dialogue occurs in Chapter 3, in a tryst of Fyodor and Zina Mertz. This is one of the problematic points where a singular feature of the narrative is noticeable.

The part of dialogue which is put in quotation marks begins as follows: "'To you it's only funny,' said Zina crossly" (192; 372). As the "it's" suggests, the narrator seems to start to record a really much longer conversation not from the beginning but from halfway, making the reader feel suddenly tossed in the middle of their dialogue. It is only when Fyodor asks toward the end of the conversation: "are we going to meet all our lives like this, side by side on a bench?" (194; 374) that the reader realizes the fact that they are talking on a bench.

It is inferable from the fact that the paragraph following this dialogue begins with the words "But a few days later" (194; 374) that the dialogue may be taken place in the evening of one particular day. A reference to this "particular day" might possibly be found way before the recitation part of the conversation (as many as 20 pages before): "In the distance a large clock . . . slowly chimed nine o'clock. It was time to go and meet Zina" (176; 356). However, what should be noticed is that their tryst scene is rendered not as what happened in one particular evening through the simple past tense but again as a repeated, habitual occurrence: the narrator tries to describe Zina's appearance in one particular moment and one specific meeting not through an usual, plain way of describing the past event but by producing accumulated images of their repeated meetings, using such expressions as: "They usually met on the other side of the railway bridge"; "She was always late" (176; 356); "She always unexpectedly appeared out of the darkness" (177; 357). After this the narrator, leaving the two lovers in this specific evening suspended for a while, starts to recollect and relate how they met, what they have talked about, how Zina grew up

−97−

and how miserable she feels both in the present family and in her office. The reader, therefore, almost forgets the fact that the narrator at the very beginning focused on one specific point of time in the past (the evening of their tryst). The narrator on one hand prepares the limited time frame of one particular evening to describe, but on the other hand presents it as a repeated evening scene, together with the events and conversations that had happened still earlier in the past. Only after the reader completely forgets about the point of departure of this meeting the narrator abruptly makes Zina utter: "To you it's only funny." The inserted conversation, therefore, seems to be quite conveniently arranged, if not really "invented," by the narrator, who wants to bring his narration back to the time of their tryst from an infinitely digressive recollection of the past events.

The reality of this dialogue becomes more questionable when we try to ascertain what the "[a]ll it" in Zina's first remark signifies. We should interpret "it" as the whole long story about herself that the narrator has just recounted in detail in the form of recollection, which seems, however, rather unrealistic: it is as if Zina, just like us, had been reading that long reminiscent narrative and then pronounced the narrative as "it." Therefore some readers (more precisely, re-reader), who have already read the invented conversation between the two artists, are inclined to suspect the same illusional nature in this seemingly natural scene of a dialogue. The two lovers communicate to and understand each other, of course, and it might be true the dialogue here is "the real communication that Fyodor and Zina have established,"[16] still we cannot part with the idea that this three-page long, too perfectly ordered dialogue on a bench might be a more or less patched and perfectly rearranged one. A bench, therefore, works in both two scenes of an important dialogue as a convenient setting, and more importantly, it signals for the readers to notice something unusual is happening in the narrative.

---

[16] Boyd, *Russian Years*, 469.

Chapter III Mapping out Fyodor's Berlin

A bench also provides a setting for the narrator to freely create an illusory vision. In the following line, for example, the narrator produces a vision by means of shadow, which makes, incidentally, a beautiful contrast to
that bench scene in the daytime square where the narrative is closely connected with the state of the sun: "... the beautiful girl who for the last
eight years had kept refusing to be incarnated ... was sitting on a cinder-
gray bench, but when he got closer he saw that only the bent shadow of
the poplar trunk was sitting there" (53; 239).

In the next excerpt Fyodor slips from the present Berlin into his family
estate in the past Russia:

> He walked along his favorite one [path] toward the still invisible
> house, past the bench on which according to established tradition
> his parents used to sit on the eve of his father's regular departures
> on his travels: Father, knees apart, twirling his spectacles or a carna-
> tion in his hands, had his head lowered, with a boater tipped onto
> the back of it and with a taciturn almost mocking smile around his
> puckered eyes and in the soft corners of his mouth, somewhere in
> the very roots of his trimmed beard; and Mother was telling him
> something, from the side, from below, from beneath her large,
> trembling white hat; or was pressing out crunchy little holes in the
> dump sand with the tip of her parasol. (79; 263)

Though we can clearly visualize his parents sitting on the bench, we also
notice a certain ambiguity of the description: we cannot determine
whether Fyodor the character is really looking at his parents now on this
bench or it is only a detailed recollection of their "established tradition" on
the part of the narrator, hence there is no one on the imagined bench.
Maybe the both are right: by the use of the "used to," the narrator tries to
describe the vision as a habitual picture, and at the same time, by minutely
describing their figures after the colon, he manages to render the impression that this is a vision perceived right there by Fyodor's eye.[17]

Like the scene of an invented dialogue, the question here is to whose

– 99 –

consciousness (Fyodor the character's or the narrator's) the described vision should be attributed. We can dismiss the matter by just interpreting
this as "his [character Fyodor's] reminiscence" (80; 264), but such a plain
reading could diminish the delight generously prepared by Nabokov for us.
We are expected to stop by the bench, to relish the detailed illustration
slowly, to be bemused by the flickering nature of this picture, being unsure
if they are really there in one's eye or just an illusion composed with light
and shadow.

The narrator (and Nabokov) prefers to defocus a specific scene in a specific moment, covering it with the narrative of a habitual, repeated scene by
using "would" and "used to." As a result, the scene set in a particular time
of a particular day is always slightly glimpsed through the multiplied veil
of a habitual past vision. This method may be associated with Nabokov's
idea of "timelessness": "I confess I do not believe in time. I like to fold my
magic carpet, after use, in such a way as to superimpose one part of the
pattern upon another" (*SM* 109). It may be possible to read this folded
"magic carpet" as Nabokov's own text: the pattern woven in a specific, focused timeframe is superimposed with the repeated, habitual pattern woven in unspecific time in the past, which denies the idea of time in the
form of a straight line, generating the image that everything exists and
happens at the same time. Fyodor's remark on the bench: "I seem to re-

---

[17] The original passage describing his parents seems much more ambiguous. The English version is composed with complete sentences with a subject and its accompanying
verb in a certain tense: "Father ... *had* his head *lowered*"; "Mother *was telling* him"
(italics are added), etc. While the Russian version here reads: " отец—расставив
колень, вертя в руках очки или гвоздику, *опустив* голову ... а мать
—*говоряшая* ему что-то ..."(the italicized parts in both versions above correspond to each other), that is, all the verbs accompanying the "father" and "mother" are
in the form similar to the English participles, which expresses in this case a state, a
condition, and not an action. Therefore in the English version his parents are described
with their movement, while the Russian version gives us the impression that they are
depicted as a static picture.

member my future works" (194; 374) then seems to suggest even the future already exists parallel with the past and the present.

Benches in other works

Let us now examine several other bench scenes found in other works in order to look at those benches in *The Gift* from varied angles. While working on this novel, Nabokov wrote the story "Recruiting" (*"Nabor"* 1935), in which he introduced an impressive way of using a bench, of which developed form is adopted in *The Gift*. The narrator, while recounting the past of an old man called V.I., gradually turns one's attention to himself, and finally suggests that what he has been talking here is his total invention, inspired by an old man sitting beside him on the bench. However, in the end the "narrator" also proves to be merely a chance representative chosen by the real author (most likely Nabokov), as this "narrator" chose the old man as a character in his story. Here also the bench serves as a special setting where the convoluted relationship among the character, the narrator and the higher creative authority and their consciousness are put into question, allowing us a further understanding of what could be happening in the bench scenes in *The Gift*.

Bench scenes in Nabokov's works are often accompanied by the effective play of light and shadow, or the sunlight, which serve to elucidate lurking problems of the complicated narrative. "Recruiting" is concluded with the following line, which is attributed to the true author (not the narrator), describing the man he chose as the narrator: "My representative, the man with the Russian newspaper, was now alone on the bench and, as he had moved over into the shade where V.I. had just been sitting, the same cool linden pattern that had anointed his predecessor now rippled across his forehead" (*Stories* 405). The narrator ends up to be interwoven with the character V.I. into the shadowy pattern of narrative that is formed by the linden and the sunlight. The narrator's remark at the beginning of

– 101 –

Reading Nabokov's Framed Landscape

the story that resigned old émigrés are "linked up by death's shame and its vulgar equality" (*Stories* 401) introduces the idea of "equality," which can be also discerned in the last line cited above, where the narrator and the character are equalized in the same sunlight. This idea has the same importance in *The Gift*, for Fyodor, when trying to recount the story about the dead Yasha Chernyshevski and his friends, pronounce that "the rays of a sun that is my own and yet is incomprehensible to me, strike them and equalize them in the same burst of light" (42; 229).

Benches continue to play significant roles also in Nabokov's English works, but let us limit the discussion to the following passage found in a capital bench scene in *Lolita*, which covers the last two paragraphs of part 1, Chapter 5: "How marvelous were my fancied adventures as I sat on a hard park bench pretending to be immersed in a trembling book. Around the quiet scholar, nymphets played freely, as if he were a familiar statue or part of an old tree's shadow and sheen" (*Lo* 20). This passage echoes that bench scene in *The Gift* where the eye of Fyodor and that of the sun alternately open. Both scenes are based on the same pattern—the protagonist on a bench with a book on his lap, in the sunlight; moreover, the book in both cases somehow ceases to be a book, possibly by the force of the sun ("an agent of transformation," to borrow Connolly's words:[18] Fyodor's book, "open in his lap, became ever heavier and more unbooklike" (60; 245), and as for Humbert, "I dissolved in the sun, with my book for fig leaf" (*Lo* 20).

In the last two paragraphs of the chapter including the passage quoted above Humbert as the narrator first evokes himself on that "hard bench" and then digresses into several other recollections about chance nymphets, and finally comes back to a scene where Humbert sits on a park bench; it is worth noting that the bench serving as the entrance of this whole passage and the bench set in its exit may not necessarily be the same one (one

---

[18] Connolly, *Early Fiction*, 212.

−102−

Chapter III Mapping out Fyodor's Berlin

might recall that yawn in *The Gift*, which is "begun by a woman in the lighted window of the first car" and is "completed by another woman—in the last one"). Also the last few lines pose again the question in whose voice the narrator speaks: "Ah, leave me alone in my pubescent park, in my mossy garden. Let them play around me forever. Never grow up" (*Lo* 21). This may be either the voice of Humbert who was sitting on that bench then or that of Humbert who is writing this now (if we choose the latter, we have to conclude that Humbert is not repentant after all).

A bench is used as a setting where the problem of the narrator's and the character's consciousness is focused already in Nabokov's earliest works. Isahaya pays attention to the word "shadow" as an allusion to the image of "double" in the poem "A Hotel Room" ("Nomer v gostinitze," 1919):[19] "Not quite a bed, not quite a bench. / Wallpaper: a grim yellow. / A pair of chairs. A squinty looking-glass. / We enter—my shadow and I." In this stanza quoted above, indeed, our eyes are inevitably attracted "I" and the reflected figure of the "I," dismissing other object such as the thing that looks "not quite a bed, not quite a bench." Though this bench / bed is of no significance by itself, when juxtaposed with the next excerpt from *Mashen'ka*, (1926; *Mary*, 1970), it suddenly becomes an eloquent and somehow suggestive device: "He sat down on a bench in a public garden and at once a gentle companion who had been following him, his gray vernal shadow, stretched out at his feet and began to talk."[20] This line shows the protagonist Ganin in a public garden (Nabokov's favored setting again), and it is clear that the combination of bench / shadow and the image of double drawn from it is a certain reproduction of the first stanza of the poem quoted above. In this scene the action of sitting on the bench

---

[19] 諫早勇一 「ナボコフのロシア語作品と分身テーマ」『言語文化』第2巻第4号, 2000年, 533 – 46, 537-8.

[20] *Mary*. Trans. Michael Glenny in collaboration with the author. 1970. New York: Vintage, 1989. 30-31.

becomes a trigger for the "shadow," the protagonist's double, to be enlivened, therefore, we could imagine that the bench in "A Hotel Room" might be already endowed with a potential for evocating the shadow, the double.

Moreover, the motif of the fusion between a bed and a bench also develops in *Mary* right after the line cited above. What the phrase "shadow . . . began to talk" actually means is that Ganin starts to recollect himself when he was recuperating from typhus nine years ago in Russia. In this recollection, Ganin in the past floats and flies out of the room on his bed, and "[a]ll day long the bed kept gliding into the hot windy sky" (*Mary* 32), so he keeps gliding in the sky of past Petersburg. However, the narrative turns back abruptly, without any sign, to a line depicting the present Ganin in Berlin, saying: "All Tuesday he wondered from square to square" (*Mary* 33). As the two lines quoted here suggest, the present Ganin and the past Ganin are depicted without any clear distinction between them. What is important here is the fact that this recollection of the bench flight begins with Ganin's sitting on the bench: the bench that holds the present Ganin is magically transformed into the bed on which the past Ganin lies. "Not quite a bed, not quite a bench" could be seen therefore a herald of this merging bed and bench in the novel.

Isahaya also suggests that the theme of double, which in the author's early works implies the protagonist's eye that regards himself as other person, develops into "an intentional mixture of the first-person and the third-person voice" in the later works.[21] Nabokov in as early as his first novel adopted a bench as a setting where the protagonist's consciousness is split into two; this bench in his first work is grown to a more complicated device that sheds light on the relations between the character's and narrator's consciousness, and its accompanying shifts of narrative voices in his last Russian novel.

---

[21] 諫早，「ナボコフのロシア語作品と分身テーマ」, 542.

Chapter III Mapping out Fyodor's Berlin

Finally, let us again take a look at the bench scenes in *The Gift* and examine Nabokov's characteristic way of rendering the past with the effective
use of the "would" and "used to," or "always," which serve to blur a particular moment in a mist of repeated or habitual state. This way of expressing
the past seems to simulate a style of Flaubert and Proust, whose usage of
past imperfect is one of Nabokov's interests and whose works Fyodor ad-
mires as well.[22] Nabokov in his lecture on *Madame Bovary* analyzes Flaubert's use of past imperfect form, "expressive of an action or state in con-
tinuance, something that has been happening in an habitual way," which in
English "is best rendered by *would* or *used to*"; he also quotes Proust's remark that "Flaubert's mastery of time, of flowing time, is expressed by his
use of the imperfect," which "enables Flaubert to express the continuity of
time and its unity" (*LL* 172). Complaining of the English translators' having neglected this style, Nabokov shows us an ideal sample translation by
himself: "She would begin [*not* "*began*"] by looking around her to see if
nothing had changed since last she had been there. She would find [*not*
"*found*"] again in the same places the foxgloves and wallflowers . . ." (*LL*
172). Some readers of *The Gift* inevitably sense an affinity between the
style of this translation and the style found, for instance, in that bench
scene where Fyodor bathes in the sun, inclining them to see those sentences written with "would" as if they had been translated from French *imparfait* sentences.[23] Thus benches in *The Gift* may be on one hand a remnant
of Russian literature, and on the other marks the scenes where the narra-

---

[22] Foster states that Fyodor "embodies Nabokov's French interests at the time of writing," clarifying the novel's relationship with Proust and Flaubert, who "Fyodor identifies with a second trend in modern European literature" (Foster, John Burt, Jr. *Nabokov's Art of Memory and European Modernism*. Princeton: Princeton UP, 1993, 148.)
[23] Kudo presented in 2007 a highly insightful reading of *Lolita*, focusing on Humbert's
use of "Flaubertian intonation." For her close examination on Nabokov's distinguished
usage of various past tenses, see *Nabokov and World Literature: Proceedings of the 2007
General Meeting of the Nabokov Society of Japan*, 31-44.

tive becomes conscious of European modern literature.

When Nabokov's specialized style of recreating the past coincides with the appearance of a bench, we could find there a scene framed in a more complicated time structure than it seems, which is of more or less the same tonality as Flaubert or Proust, but is developed into a unique form to express Nabokov's own singular concept of time as well. Benches continue to appear all through the later works as a landmark in critical points where the reader could find some secrets of Nabokov's narrative style. More importantly, Nabokov successfully made benches into a kind of time-traveling-machine which creates a special texture of time.

Chapter IV
Following Fyodor's Footsteps

1. The Post Office: Entrance

Though it transpired that producing a whole map of *The Gift* seems impossible, it also means that if we carefully keep following Fyodor's steps we may discover unexpected paths limitlessly diverging from the main road. In this chapter we will take a thorough walk with Fyodor, in hope of identifying the work under the title "a pedestrian novel." As Stephen H. Blackwell suggests, *The Gift* "continues the great Russian tradition of street poems: 'The Bronze Horseman,' 'Nevski Avenue' (and most of the 'Petersburg Tales'), *Crime and Punishment, Petersburg...*," [1] it is worth focusing on those elusive streets appearing and then disappearing in *The Gift* and, above all, the act of walking itself. We will explore how "walking" plays a dominant role in *The Gift*, with special focus on the motif of entrance/exit, which seems to belong to the wider category of a "street" or "walking" theme.

We enter this novel from "Tannenberg Street" that is described as "beginning with a post office and ending with a church, like an epistolary novel" (4; 192). This is not a mere simile: although *The Gift* is not what we traditionally call an "epistolary novel," we will notice the novel is replete with "epistolary" motifs. Before examining the entrance theme, therefore,

---

[1] Blackwell, Stephen H. *Zina's Paradox: The Figured Reader in Nabokov's* The Gift. New York: Peter Lang, 2000, 145.

– 107 –

we must step into a secret byway of "the letter theme," regarding this post office as the first secret entrance; considering the wildly discursive nature of the novel, a little digression on our part would be allowed.[2] We will re-read the novel by focusing first on the correspondence between Fyodor and his mother, secondly on N. G. Chernyshevski's letters quoted by Fyodor, and thirdly on Fyodor's last letter to his mother, which will be our main concern here.

Before we proceed to *The Gift*, we have to clarify principal features of letters in Nabokov's works. Firstly, they often turn out to be one-way letters: to put it differently, in many cases, the receiver of a letter is in a sense absent, or at least, indeterminate. The obvious examples are "Ultima Thule,"[3] in which the addressee is the narrator's dead wife, and "A Letter That Never Reached Russia,"[4] the "never reached" in the English title implying the lack of a receiver.

In *Despair*, while the narrator and protagonist, Herman Karlovich, willingly quotes the letters written by himself, he never tries to show the original letters from Felix, saying "all the *answers* have been destroyed."[5] It might be said that this is a variation of "one-way letters."

In *Pale Fire*, Kinbote shows us a letter to his wife, in which he mentions a letter from her. Her letter in question, however, is never presented

---

[2] Kopper observes the "recurrence of letters in Nabokov's prose" reveals "the importance he accorded them in the construction of plot." "Letters," he continues, "help Nabokov's characters break open the chambers of solitude where time and space confine the human soul." See Kopper, John M., "Correspondence," in *The Garland Companion to Vladimir Nabokov.*, ed. Vladimir E. Alexandrov (New York: Garland, 1995), 54-67. Also Brian Boyd's treatment to "letters theme" in his *Nabokov's Ada: The Place of Consciousness* (Ann Arbor: Ardis, 1985. Rev. ed, Christchurch, NZ: Cyhbereditions, 2001) confirms the importance of letters in Nabokov's work.

[3] Nabokov, Vladimir. "Ultima Thule," in *The Stories of Vladimir Nabokov* (1995. New York: Vintage, 1997), 500-522.

[4] *Stories*, 137-140.

[5] *Despair*. 1966. London: Penguin, 2000, 57. Henceforth as *Des*.

Chapter IV Following Fyodor's Footsteps

to us, as if it did not exist at all. Nabokov states in his commentary on *Eugene Onegin* that the epistolary form of novels "necessitates the author's providing his main characters with confidants" (*EO* II 341). This is a simple, and at the same time highly important, rule when viewed in the context of Nabokov's works: Nabokov quite often refuses to provide his characters with confidants.

Roman Bogdanovich in *The Eye* is believed to send a letter every Friday to a "Tallin friend," whose existence seems rather doubtful: he says elsewhere that the supposed reader of these letters is the "very old" Roman Bogdanovich of the future[6] and he complains, when his letter is intercepted by the narratorial "I," or Smurov, "'Perhaps I had no intention to post it. . .'" (*Eye* 82). The archetype of Roman Bogdanovich can be detected in Goethe's *Die Leiden des jungen Werthers*, a novel which "is mostly in epistolary form," explains Nabokov in his commentary on *Eugene Onegin*, "consisting of letters—really monologues—addressed by Werther to a certain Wilhelm, who mercifully remains mute and invisible" (*EO* II 345). "A monologue disguised as a letter" may be the precise expression for those letters (letter-shaped stories included) mentioned above.

Another example is the narrator of *The Eye*, who "wanted to write a few traditional letters" before committing suicide, but finds that he "had no one to write to" because he "knew few people and loved no one" (*Eye* 17).[7] There are many such characters who lack their correspondent. For Nabokov characters, in other words, having a confidant to write to is a big comfort and happiness. It is also probable that some characters, pretending not to be alone and lonely, try to write letters to "mute," "invisible," vague

---

[6] *The Eye*. Trans. Dmitri Nabokov in collaboration with the author, 1965, New York: Vintage, 1990, 77. Henceforth as *Eye*.

[7] "[A] few traditional letters" before committing suicide remind us of the three letters Charlotte writes before she is killed, which we will discuss later in this essay. "Three letters" are passim, and the "destroyed" three letters from Felix, which are mentioned in this paper, are one of them.

– 109 –

correspondents. Letters in Nabokov's works thus prove frequently not to be a means of normal communication.

Secondly, letters are sometimes seen as diaries and as a means of "self-preservation." The idea is clearly observed in the expression "epistolary diary" in *The Eye*. Roman Bogdanovich stays home every Friday "to write his diary," and he insists that it gives him "a feeling of self-preservation," saying, "you preserve your entire life, and, in later years, rereading it, you may find it not devoid of fascination" (*Eye* 76); he is supposed to send "weekly contributions" to a "Tallin Friend" (*Eye* 77). This has something to do with the problem to whom a letter is written, or, more generally, for whom a book is written. For instance, it is sometimes suggested that the supposed reader of *The Gift* is the future Fyodor himself.

Thirdly, let us focus our attention on "coded" letters. It seems that letters in Nabokov's works are supposed to be read by a stranger, not by the intended reader. The most well-known case is the correspondence between Ada and Van, which is written in their own invented code.[8] We can find other minor references to a "code" in places. For example, *The Eye* has a scene in which the narrator reads by stealth a letter from "a certain Uncle Pasha" to Khrushchov, expecting to find some allusion to Smurov; it turns out there is none, and he says, "if it was coded, then I did not know the key" (*Eye* 58).

We may say that the theme of "coded letters" is linked to that of "translated letters." The origin of this theme is, no doubt, Tatiana's letter to Onegin, which is supposed to have been written in French but "translated" by Pushkin into Russian. Again in *Despair*, Herman "remembers" and reproduces the third letter among the three "destroyed" letters from Felix, explaining, "I was long in relishing that last letter, the Gothic charm of which my rather tame translation is hardly capable of rendering" (*Des* 104). The same device is adopted by Humbert Humbert, who remembers and

---

[8] *Ada, or Ardor: A family Chronicle.* 1969. New York: Vintage, 1990.

Chapter IV Following Fyodor's Footsteps

recreates Charlotte's "destroyed" letter (*Lo* 67-69). Humbert, as Wood aptly describes, "is only translating, or recreating," therefore, Charlotte's letter can also be seen as "translated."[9] Coded letters and translated letters are very close, for they are both rephrased from the original (as for "translated" ones, however, the original is an "illusion," that is, nonexistent, as Wood points out).[10] Letters in Nabokov's works are thus doomed to be decoded and reconstructed, and sometimes mercilessly, selfishly interpreted, abridged, and translated by others, including us, the readers of his works.

Fourthly, we notice the curious fact that letters are often accompanied with a strong wind. We are familiar with at least two scenes in which a man holding a letter (or letters) is struggling with an extraordinarily violent wind: in the aforementioned scene in which Smurov intercepts Roman Bogdanovich's letter, an unusually strong wind keeps buffeting the street; Chapter 3 of *Despair* begins with the image of a postman, who first "walks backwards" and later "has swerved round and, bent double, still fighting, walks forward" in "the wind's violence" (*Des* 45).[11] We could interpret in several ways the image of a letter in a strong wind, but if seen quite simply, it seems to imply the difficulties a letter might go through before reaching the intended address.

The last point we emphasize is that letters bearing a date can provide the reader with chronological information. Chapter 4 of *Despair* opens with the whole text of Herman's letter, which is followed by the statement: "Here it is before me, the letter I finally wrote on that ninth of September, 1930" (*Des* 57). After this, while explaining the features of an "epistolic

---

[9] Wood, Michael. *The Magician's Doubts: Nabokov and the Risks of Fiction*, (Princeton: Princeton UP, 1995), 118.

[10] Ibid., 145.

[11] The wind, like other meteorological motifs, repeatedly appears in Nabokov's works, partly as an indicator of the Maker's (or the author's) presence (of course, there are many other explanations on the matter), so the "wind-letter" pair is only a part of the wind theme.

form of narration," he assures the readers that they will "find the date" above each quoted letter, and continues: "Dates are required . . . to keep up the illusion" (*Des* 58). When reading a work by Nabokov, indeed, dates on letters are always helpful to reconstruct the chronology of the work. We have, for example, a dated letter from Lolita in Part 2, Chapter 27, which serves to establish, though at the same time to confuse, the timeline of *Lolita*.

Incidentally, the following passage found in the comment on an "epistolic form of narration" mentioned above is noteworthy: "all those 'do-you-remember-that-time-whens" (detailed recollections follow) are brought in, not so much with the object of refreshing Why's memory as in order to give the reader the required reference . . ." (*Des* 58). This remark immediately reminds us of "Ultima Thule," which actually begins with the phrase "Do you remember the day . . ." (*Stories* 500). Also the opening paragraph of "A Letter That Never Reached Russia" consists of a detailed memory of the shared past of two lovers (*Stories* 137).

Having glanced at the main features of letters in Nabokov's works, touching only a few examples, we may now turn our attention to the numerous other letters contained within *The Gift*, each of which deserves careful scrutiny.

Correspondence between Mother and Son

As mentioned before, we will take a close look firstly at the correspondence between Fyodor and his mother, secondly at the fragments from Chernyshevski's letters, and thirdly at Fyodor's last and possibly the most significant letter to his mother.

Let us add another feature of Nabokov letters here: letters are often presented as a sample of a respective character's writings. Nabokov in his commentary on *Eugene Onegin* tells us, "In the course of the novel Pushkin quotes the writings of all three main characters: Tatiana's letter, Lenski's last elegy, and Onegin's letter" (*EO* II 384), and we know Nabokov himself

Chapter IV Following Fyodor's Footsteps

adopts the device in his own works by quoting articles, books and letters written by his characters. In *The Gift*, we can get some idea of the writing style of the protagonist, and of his mother, through their letters.

As already stated, letters in Nabokov's works cannot be regarded as a means of communication in many cases. They seem to be wandering, with no address to reach. Correspondence between Fyodor and his mother, however, appears to be an exception: it is an ideal communication, with the son's inquiries and the mother's prompt replies flowing smoothly.[12] However, it is not presented in the text only to show their ideal relationship: the letters are deliberately woven into the right spots within the text. As Píchová points out, fragments of his mother's letters are set to frame the biography of his father.[13] Their letters implanted there, at the beginning and the ending of his father's biography, look as if they were a part of an epistolary novel. His mother, as a good adviser, encourages Fyodor to write his first prose work, replying immediately to his questions with words that never disappoint him. Their conversation-like letters thus form a part of the biography. The important point to note is that there is no gap between each fragment of their letters: Fyodor's question is immediately followed by his mother's answer, which ignores and resolves the actual space and time separating mother and son. At least in the text, a long blank in which one waits for the other's letter mercifully disappears. The flow of the correspondence creates the impression of a dialogue unfolding in a single place and time, its continuity uninterrupted. These fragments of their letters, moreover, are all free from dates (except for the one Fyodor writes on his father's birthday), which encourages us to ignore the entire

---

[12] The mother and the son indeed seem to understand each other unusually well, so that their "conversation" gives us the impression that they should really be the same person, as the case of the invented dialogues between Fyodor and Koncheyev.

[13] Píchová, Hana. *The Art of Memory in Exile: Vladimir Nabokov and Milan Kundera*, (Southern Illinois UP, 2002), 43. Here she regards letters as one of the other fragments which are expected to "evoke personal memories."

space / time lag. In this correspondence we find the happiness of having a correspondent, the happiness of sharing memories and the happiness of understanding each other. Their ideal correspondence, more precisely, one of his mother's letters, act as the catalyst to launch Fyodor's first prose writing.

Fyodor as a reader of Chernyshevski's letters

Next, let us focus on the letters of N. G. Chernyshevski, a historical figure and the protagonist in "The Life of Chernyshevski," Fyodor's first complete work of prose. Although Fyodor ridicules and caricatures Chernyshevski, his way of treating Chernyshevski's letters sometimes strikes us as sincere and even compassionate. In this biography Fyodor analyzes large numbers of letters and concludes that they are "the letters of a model youth." He continues: "instead of imagination he was prompted by his obliging good nature as to what another would relish" (218-19; 397). For example, he keeps feeding his father, "who liked all sorts of events," with news, information about fads and so on. Here, Fyodor shows us examples of these historical events, using Nabokov's famous "tabulation device." His letters, therefore, can be regarded as a means to getting to know the life and incidents of those days. More noteworthy is the word "imagination" in his comment on Chernyshevski's style in letters. It implies Chernyshevski's lack of imagination in all respects, and moreover, it suggests Fyodor's belief that even a letter should be written with a certain degree of imagination. Indeed, Fyodor writes his own letter with imagination, especially the last one in the novel.

The presentation of Chernyshevski's letters to his father is followed by observations on his letters from Siberia to his wife and children, which gradually encourage Fyodor to evoke and delineate the profile of his protagonist. From these letters Fyodor constructs the image of Chernyshevski, consolidating it with his predilection, his habits and so on.

– 114 –

Chapter IV Following Fyodor's Footsteps

The most critical letter of all is the one with a trace of Chernyshevski's tear. Fyodor presents the letter in the following manner: "Before us is Chernyshevski's famous letter to his wife dated December 5, 1862: a yellow diamond among the dust of his numerous works" (273; 449). His remark here, though ironical, nevertheless seems to ascribe at least a greater value to the letter than any other works by Chernyshevski (actually none of his works attracts Fyodor). He continues to analyze the letter closely, from his handwriting to the trace of a tear, with possibly the same passion with which he would analyze a work of art. Here, he also tells us that Chernyshevski's fictional biographer, Strannolyubski, "justly designates this letter as the beginning of Chernyshevski's brief flowering" (273; 449). The quotation from Strannolyubski seems to justify Fyodor's special focus on this letter and moreover leads to the idea that the letter is important also as the starting-point of Chernyshevski's creative period. That the highly private writings of a man to his wife could be preserved for the thorough scrutiny of an utter stranger in the future serves to underline the capacity for even private correspondence to be decoded and eventually judged as art by others. This is what happens when "Ultima Thule" and "A Letter That Never Reached Russia" are read. Therefore this idea of a private letter as a work of art must always be active in Nabokov's mind. Fyodor's treatment of letters here reminds us of this concept of Nabokov, and we will later explore Fyodor's last letter with the same curiosity and passion as Fyodor's.

Before that, some other important letters of Chernyshevski should be briefly mentioned. Fyodor next closely examines Chernyshevski's "second letter to his wife" written two days after the first one, and this is followed by the remark "A few days after that he began to write his novel *What to Do?*"(274; 450). The process above makes it clear that these two letters can be regarded as the introduction to his most famous work. It can be said that writing these letters motivated him to write the novel. As correspondence between Fyodor and his mother became the entrance to his father's biography, Chernyshevski's letters to his wife became the starting-

－115－

point of his novel.

The letters from which Fyodor quotes are all written by Chernyshevski, thus we are not sure whether his wife and children wrote to him or not. There is only one exception—a letter from Chernyshevski's father advising his son to write "some tale or other" (288; 464). While Fyodor himself cannot receive letters from his father any more, Chernyshevski gets at least one letter from his father. The brief paragraph in which Fyodor comments on the letter from Chernyshevski's father seems not very important at first glance. However, Fyodor, by quoting his protagonist's father, seems to try to alleviate Chernyshevski's loneliness. Fyodor thus proves that not all Chernyshevski's letters were one-way letters. Chernyshevski, unlike Fyodor, receives an encouraging letter from his father, which is a fact Fyodor cannot overlook. We may presume that Fyodor, in writing this paragraph, shows his compassion for Chernyshevski.

On reading Chernyshevski's letter, what catches Fyodor's attention is the "pure sound" of the letter, which cannot be heard in Chernyshevski's fiction. The following phrases Fyodor extracts contain several key words and expressions that permeate *The Gift* itself:

> "My dearest darling, I thank you for being the light of my life." . . .
> "I would be even here one of the happiest men in the world if it did not occur to me that this fate, which is very much to my personal advantage, is too hard in its effects on your life, my dear friend." . . .
> "Will you forgive me the grief to which I have subjected you?" (287; 462)

It is notable that these fragments embrace such dominant ideas in *The Gift* as "happiness," "thanks" and "fate." This "pure sound," however, rings with a pitiful note, because there is no reference to a reply from his wife at all. The reader is not sure whether these selfless, sincere words really reached Chernyshevski's wife's heart. His wife, the only intended reader of his letters, might not appreciate them, might be unable to make out the "pure sound," while Fyodor, an utter stranger, in her stead reads them carefully

Chapter IV Following Fyodor's Footsteps

and generously rescues these pure words to eternalize in his text. Chernyshevski's letters to his wife seem to be completely ignored by his wife, but
Fyodor mercifully responds to them as if to compensate her cruel silence.

Fyodor in his biography of Chernyshevski treats letters carefully to extract the essence out of them. As he analyzes the letters of his protagonist,
we will now explore our protagonist's most important letter.

A Letter That Never Reached . . .

In reading Chapter 4 ("The Life of Chernyshevski") in which Fyodor scru-
tinizes his protagonist's letters, we ourselves may consequently become inclined to take a close look at Fyodor's own letters, and in so doing may
find an ideal object of study in Chapter 5: his lengthy letter to his mother.
On rereading it closely, we will discover, as expected, many factors that
would enrich the world of *The Gift*. We could even call it Fyodor's hidden
"yellow diamond" (sincerely, not ironically) but unlike Chernyshevski's, his
letter is highly imaginative. Correspondence between Fyodor and his
mother, as discussed in the previous section, can be seen as a successful
means of communication. The last letter to his mother, however, is quite
different from the other letters: it is not so much "conversation" as a
monologue, through which the reader hears Fyodor's true voice.

Fyodor the narrator almost abruptly begins to quote this letter, without
explaining this is Fyodor the character's letter to his mother. The reader
will find no line that should indicate this is a letter, and also no reply from
his mother that can be seen, but the occasional use of "you" gradually encourages the reader to presume this must be Fyodor's letter to his mother.
Here, we will observe this imaginative, but somehow inchoate, letter, from
four different angles.

The first point to notice is a certain link (or analogy) between a letter
and a phone call—a link found in many works by Nabokov. The theme of
"collaboration of letters and the telephone" surely permeates *The Gift*, and

– 117 –

we will first clarify the analogy between these two media of communication. At the beginning of the letter Fyodor writes, "The other day I wrote Tanya a long, lyrical letter, but I have an uncomfortable feeling that I put the wrong address on it: instead of '122' I put some other number, without thinking, just as I did once before" (348-49; 524). This remark reminds us of a man who always calls up the Shchyogolevs by mistake "because of the similarity of the [telephone] numbers" (156-57; 337). Fyodor himself eventually makes the same mistake (325; 500). The theme of "wrong number," therefore, connects address of a letter and telephone numbers. This theme also leads us to the theme of "wandering letters," which we will discuss later.

We may note, in passing, that several interesting images lurk in the number "122." For example, when it is placed in reverse order, it will be transformed to a famous address in the world of fiction: 221B Baker Street where Sherlock Holmes lived.[14] "122" also corresponds with the special figures that appear in Proust's *À La Recherche du temps perdu*. In "Noms de pays: le noms," Marcel seems to be possessed by "le beau train généreux d'une heur vingt-deux."[15] The Number 1.22, which signifies the time of departure of the "generous train," is therefore a magic number that would bring him to the cities of which he dreams. It is also interesting to note that Marcel and Fyodor seem to be in a common situation more or less. Though 122 must be a magic number that symbolizes Marcel's dream

---

[14] Though the reference to Doyle's detective here may sound irrelevant, Holmes stories, mentioned sometimes in Nabokov's work, share certain ideas with *The Gift*: a biographer who tries to recapture the image of his close person, and the impossible return of a once killed man. Incidentally, in *The Return of Sherlock Holmes*, narrated by Watson as the detective's biographer, Holmes is back to 221B Baker Street, disguised as an old bookseller with a curved back, who bears a vague resemblance to the old, long-nosed book peddler with a bent back, who sells books to Chernyshevski (243).

[15] Proust, Marcel. *À la recherche du temps perdu, Du côté de chez Swann*, édition présentée et annotée par Antoine Compagnon, (Paris: Gallimard, 1987-88), 378.

Chapter IV Following Fyodor's Footsteps

cities including Balbec, he, rather passive in everything, is always doubtful of the idea of really catching this train. So it will take quite a long time for him to decide to take this special train. This number thus remains for Marcel only a dream number for a while. For Fyodor, "122" means the address at which his family lives—the place he dreams of visiting. However, his tone in the following lines curiously resembles Marcel's passive tone when he expresses only his wish in the past, not his current intention: "I'll visit you in Paris. Generally speaking I'd abandon tomorrow this country, oppressive as a headache—where everything is alien and repulsive to me" (350; 525).[16] His idea of visiting Paris is just an idea, so we are not sure if he really leaves or not.

Now let us return to our main concern. After finishing his letter to his mother Fyodor falls asleep, when someone rings the Shchyogolevs, which later proves to be the same man who always dials the wrong number. It is also important that this very phone call eventually helps Fyodor reunite with his father in his "dream."

Nabokov's works contain numerous scenes in which letters and telephones take turns in working. In *Bend Sinister*, for example, Krug tries to call Ember in order to inform him of Olga's death. First he complains, punning, "I could never remember Ember's number."[17] Again there occurs a problem of tricky numbers (here figures are closely connected to a person. Krug observes that the "6" in the middle of his number resembles Ember's Persian nose. We may also notice that the name "Ember" has a "b" in the middle, which curiously resembles a "6"). When Krug finally seems to reach Ember, the narrative, instead of tuning into a telephone conversation as expected, abruptly turns into a long text in quotation marks, which turns out to be Ember's letter to the Maximovs. The letter

---

[16] This passage echoes with Marcel's following remark: "J'aurais voulu prendre dès le lendemain le beau train généreux d'une heur vingt-deux" (*Rechérche*, 378).
[17] *Bend Sinister*. 1947. Vintage, 1990, 27.

−119−

Reading Nabokov's Framed Landscape

shows us the fact that Ember's letter was interrupted by the phone call, so this letter is forced to change its subject into quite an unexpected one because of one call announcing Olga's death.[18]

Another memorable phone call is the one which informs Humbert of Charlotte's death (*Lo* 95-97). He is told through the phone that she had an accident, while he believes she is still in the room finishing her letters. Letters and the telephone again work together, and what should be noted is the fact that Humbert is informed not directly but indirectly about the accident that happened just outside his residence. Realistically, he would be told directly by his neighbor, therefore the telephone, literally remote especially in this context, looks like an unlikely device for telling him about the nearby accident. The same observation applies to Charlotte's third of her three letters she has just finished before she is killed. The letter, Humbert presumes, is meant for him, so if it is true she tried to send it to him via the mail service, rather than just leaving it in the room, which would have been the more likely thing for her to do. An indirect message from Charlotte, together with the indirect information about her death, make the reader recognize the theme of a "message sent in a roundabout way."[19]

Now let us go back to the telephone ringing after Fyodor wrote the letter to his mother. The phone call is transformed in his sleep into a call from his former landlady, and it eventually leads him to the dream in which his father comes back safe and sound. If the Nabokovian habit of the telephone announcing death is applicable here, this call may be work-

---

[18] It is worth noting that Nabokov frequently uses the telephone to inform his characters of someone's death. Incidentally, in reality, as in fiction, it was a phone call that informed Nabokov's family of the death of his father: in *Speak, Memory*, Nabokov's mother's speech is interrupted by the ring, and the author only uses the simple phrase "when the telephone rang," not making any further explanation (*SM* 49).

[19] The reader of *Bend Sinister* is formally informed of Olga's death in still more roundabout way, through Ember's letter briefly mentioned in this paper, not even through Krug's voice in their telephone conversation.

– 120 –

Chapter IV Following Fyodor's Footsteps

ing as a confirmation of his father's death, and of his continuing existence
too.

Secondly, we will see how this letter becomes the starting point, or an
entrance, of *The Gift* itself. Like Ember's letter mentioned above, Fyodor's
letter is also interrupted by Zina, his lover. It should not be overlooked
that the very line interrupted by her predicts a future book, which looks
exactly like *The Gift* itself. This letter, therefore, is the hidden core of this
novel. One purpose of this letter is to tell his mother how happy he is
about the birth of his sister's baby, and his remark toward the end of the
letter that "all this has something to do in a roundabout way with Tanya's
baby" (351; 526), implying a pleasant excitement derived from a new-born
life, might suggest the germ of a novel conceived in Fyodor himself. In
this one-and-a-half-page letter replete with his honest feelings about Berlin, his views on the past, present, future, and above all, on Russia, we make
out "the pure sound" of Fyodor's mind. Representing his unreserved
thoughts, this is possibly the only written source through which the reader
glimpses Fyodor's mind. This letter, which contains "non-stop trains of
thought" (351; 526), seems to be heading directly for a future book that
looks like *The Gift*. Added to the incomplete biography of his father and
Chernyshevski's *What to Do?*, *The Gift* itself has its hidden entrance in a
letter. It is important that the letter is not just a means for Fyodor to talk
about the future book to his mother, but its rhythm (most possibly the
"nocturnal rhythm" of the rain that keeps falling while he writes the letter)
of this letter seems to flow directly into the text of *The Gift*.

Thirdly, we will focus on the image of "infinity" in this letter. The letter,
quoted entirely from the begging to the end, ends in a vague, strange manner. The last part reads as follows: "Well, that's it. Keep well, *je t'embrasse.*
Night, rain quietly falling—it has found its nocturnal rhythm, and can now
go on for infinity" (351; 526). The French closing, curiously enough, is followed by one more line, and this "last" line, overflowing the traditional
closing phrase, looks slightly unusual for a remark in a letter. As the last

– 121 –

word "infinity" beautifully implies, this letter seems to continue forever, ignoring any boundary, flowing directly into the narrative of *The Gift*. The quotation mark that indicates the end of the letter is put after the line beginning with the word "Night" and ending with "infinity," but it would be more natural if it were placed after "*je t'embrasse.*" However, this unnatural ending is surely clever and necessary, for it successfully veils the boundaries between the letter and the narrative to augment the image of an infinite letter. False ending and infinite continuation are both the significant images which are found throughout the novel, as Blackwell points out: "This 'boundlessness' is Fyodor's fervently sought ideal. And this image, of course, mirrors exactly the structure of *The Gift's* composition: it is the presentation of a line that extends infinitely past the narrative boundaries."[20] It is especially important that the end of *The Gift* seems to mimic the end of the letter in question. It is no exaggeration to say that the last phrase of the novel "nor does this terminate the phrase" (366; 541) has its origin in the last part of Fyodor's letter. Once the boundaries between the letter and the novel are blurred, this letter begins to look more and more like an open entrance to the novel.

Last but not least, we must underscore the presence of the word "night," framing both the beginning and the ending of the letter; more precisely, the word "night" appears first in the line immediately before the first sentence of the letter (thus outside the letter) and then in the last sentence of the letter (thus inside it). The arrangement of this word attracts the reader's interest, and one feels like exploring this rather mysterious appearance of the night. Here, we will survey the letter on the supposition that the "night" is a latent lover of Fyodor. First, let us prove the striking contrast between Zina, his true lover, and the "Night," by emphasizing the image of "to enter."

As briefly mentioned before, the pivotal sentence that delineates his fu-

---

[20] Blackwell, *Zina's Paradox*, 159.

Chapter IV Following Fyodor's Footsteps

ture book is interrupted by Zina, and her interruption is described as follows: "The door suddenly opened, Zina half entered and without letting
go of the door handle threw something on his desk" (349; 525). Blackwell
underscores Zina's "profound respect for boundaries, which may not be
broken", and this observation is well applicable to the present scene of her
modest interruption.[21] With this in mind, let us turn to the passage followed by the first sentence of the letter:

> When supper was over and Zina had gone down to let the guests in,
> Fyodor retreated noiselessly to his room, where everything was ani-
> mated by rain and wind. He half-closed the casements of his win-
> dow, but a moment later the night said: "No," and with a kind of
> wide-eyed insistence, disdaining blows, entered again. (348; 524)

It is not too fantastic to make out the contrast between the personified
night who "entered" his room and Zina, who only "half entered." Night,
easily crossing over the boundaries, enters Fyodor's room to watch him
writing beside him, while Zina can neither enter his room nor can she
know what he is actually writing.

We discover the possible archetype of this mild confrontation between
the real lover and the "night," another lover, in "A Letter That Never
Reached Russia," a story Nabokov wrote more than ten years before *The
Gift*. The story, just like "Ultima Thule," has the form of a letter written by
a Russian writer living in exile in Berlin. The letter, overtly addressed to
his former lover in Russia, principally consists of detailed pictures of Berlin
at night. The main part of the letter begins with the brief line "It is night"
(*Stories* 137), and this Berlin night remains central until the end. Though
it may be too obvious, it should be emphasized that the line "It is night"
has the same tone as the last line (beginning with "Night,") of Fyodor's
letter in question. The following line may give authenticity to the idea of
the night as the author's other lover: "And meanwhile, outside the door,

---

[21] Blackwell, *Zina's Paradox*, 158.

waits my faithful, my lonely night with its moist reflections, hooting cars, and gusts of high-blowing wind" (*Stories* 139). It is clear through such a phrase as "my faithful, my lonely night" that the author of this letter regards the night as a girl friend. This image is clearer in the Russian original, for the noun " ночь ," "night," is feminine. The reader cannot help feeling a little abashed when encountering this sentence, realizing that there are two heroines in the story and the letter; moreover, we have the impression that the author of this letter seems to have given up his true lover in Russia in favor of the Berlin night, his new love.

Similarly in the last paragraph of the story we slightly sense the appearance of night as a lover. The paragraph opens as follows:

> Listen: I am ideally happy. My happiness is a kind of challenge. As I wander along the streets and the squares and the paths by the canal, absently sensing the lips of dampness through my worn soles, I carry proudly my ineffable happiness. (*Stories* 140)

The image that this passage creates in our mind is that the writer is kissed by "the lips" of the damp night. Curiously, in the first paragraph of the letter the writer recollects how they (he and his love) kissed on a Petersburg morning. Therefore, the first and the last paragraph vaguely echo each other, through the kiss motif. The story, incidentally, is framed with other common motifs: a loving young couple and a watchman at the opening, and a loving old couple and a watchman at the end. In addition, what should not be ignored is the feeling of "happiness." The author in the past in the first paragraph must naturally be happy with his lover, but the present author in the last paragraph is also "ineffab[ly] happy," despite his lover's absence.

All these details promote the contrast between the remote, unreachable, almost invisible, lover and the very close, intimate new love—the Berlin night. The tone of the letter must make his lover, the only intended lover, irritable and sad, feeding her with the impression that he has deserted her. It is possible that this letter should also be written on the presupposition

Chapter IV Following Fyodor's Footsteps

that it will neither be read nor even reach the addressee, as is often the case
with a Nabokovian letter. The author of the letter begins to write it, thinking that he still has a dear person to write to, but what he writes gradually
reveals his complete loneliness, with a tinge of happiness, fortunately. The
author thus eventually confronts "loneliness," the last word of this letter.

In Fyodor's last letter the sense of loneliness and the monologue-like
tone are weaker, and the night / lover association is less obvious; therefore
at first glance it is an ordinary letter to his mother. However, as the image
of the night, or more precisely "rainy night" that frames the letter indicates,
this letter slightly reverberates with the remaining tone, rhythm and senti-
ments from "A Letter That Never Reached Russia."

Fyodor's letter is interrupted by Zina, his true girlfriend, but he soon
resumes writing it, as if nobody interrupted him. Amazingly, there seems
to be no visible trace of Zina in this letter: what is stressed here is his
"wonderful solitude" (350; 526), while Zina is not directly mentioned, as if
she did not exist.[22]

What should be especially noted is the fact that Fyodor's last letter in
this novel, composed in the presence of the personified night, seems not to
be posted. The next morning Fyodor leaves his room to see the Shchyogolevs off, without bringing anything with him but three and a half marks,
and then he realizes he is unable to enter the apartment, because both his
and Zina's keys are inside it. Judging from the above, realistically speaking,
his letter will be left there in his room forever: as the last word predicts,
the words in the letter will keep wandering infinitely, without reaching

---

[22] The presence of Zina is of course important, as Salehar's early article shows (Salehar,
Anna Maria. "Nabokov's *Gift*: An Apprenticeship in Creativity" in *A Book of Things
about Vladimir Nabokov*. (Ed. Carl R. Proffer. Ardis: Ann Arbor, 1974), 70-83. They
are, as Barabtarlo observes, of course "the happiest couple of all Nabokov's couples" and
"would marry 'beyond the skyline of the page'"; but "in the projected continuation Zina
was scheduled to die." See Barabtarlo, Gennady. *Aerial View: Essays on Nabokov's Art
and Metaphysics*. New York: P. Lang, 1993, 235.

anywhere. It turns out to be a letter that never reaches his mother, so it is only the reader of the novel *The Gift* and "night" who manage to read it.

Even if this letter is neither read nor replied to by his mother, it receives a generous response in an unexpected form—a dream of his father's return. At night, after finishing his letter, he falls asleep, listening to the "whisper of the rain"—the sound which has kept accompanying Fyodor's letter, and possibly, the sound of "night's" own voice. Finally, prompted by the phone call, he plunges into the mysterious nocturnal street. Walking along, Fyodor finds "his street," which seems to be the same as the one where his first apartment in the novel was located, that is, the one that begins with a post office and ends with a church. At the end of the street "a post with a gauntleted hand on it indicated that one had to enter from the other end where the post office was," but Fyodor is "afraid of losing it in the course of a detour and moreover the post office—that would come afterwards—if Mother had not *already* been sent a telegram" (353; 529). This rather preposterous passage, based on dream logic, surely has something to do with the letter to his mother he has just finished. He needs to find the post office anyway. Fyodor, ignoring the sign, enters his street, and is at last reunited with his father. We may say that the dream of his father's return is a response from "night." The Berlin night, disguised as "the St. Petersburg white nights" (352; 528), mercifully and silently responds to Fyodor's question "when will we return to Russia?" (350; 526) and leads him to the miraculous place where he can meet his father. It seems reasonable to suppose that the Berlin night allows him to reunite with his father, maybe as a mark of gratitude to Fyodor, who generously let her (night) enter his room to stay there while he wrote the letter and, moreover, while he even mentioned her at the end of the letter.

The last letter that is unlikely to reach anywhere thus forms a focal point for the attention of a reader of *The Gift*. We realize how the Berlin night, the letter's hidden heroine and one of Fyodor's readers, plays a significant role here. The night, as the only reader of the last letter besides us,

Chapter IV Following Fyodor's Footsteps

gently and quickly responds to Fyodor's missive. There are still many letters wandering in Nabokov's works, searching for an ideal reader who, like the Berlin night, can appreciate them and give the right, responsible reply.

Letters that never reach to the intended place in Nabokov's works suggest not only the uncertainty of the address but also a certain disconnection between two places—the letter-writer's city and the addressee's, which reminds us of those isolated squares unrelated to each other. Letters, therefore, serve to clarify (or rather mystify) the nature of geography of his work.

2. Discovering Entrances

Though we have found a hidden entrance of the novel in Fyodor's last letter, we still have to turn to other entrances of *The Gift* as well. Now let us go back to the first few pages of the book. The first day and the last day of *The Gift* end almost identically: with the protagonist locked out of his apartment. Fyodor cannot enter his apartment because the key is left inside the building. As this fact already implies, "enter" and "entrance" are the key motifs to enter this story. A good place to start the argument is the following description: "The avenue had returned from the park for the night, and its entrance was shrouded in dusk" (10; 197). This line appears at the opening of Fyodor's reviews of his own work *Poems*. Though we temporarily call this "Fyodor's reviews," the matter is really convoluted, so a few remarks should be made concerning the shifts of narrative voice here. The narrator at first through the third person shows Fyodor the protagonist on the couch in his locked room reading his poems "in three dimensions" (9; 197) and reconstructing "absolutely everything" of his childhood by carefully exploring each poem. This narration imperceptibly and smoothly changes into a kind of cross between a review by Fyodor's imagined critic and a recollection of his childhood, with the smooth shift from third to first person. Such a transition occurs throughout the novel, as

Reading Nabokov's Framed Landscape

Blackwell precisely explains: "The tendency in *The Gift* is toward discontinuity, but one that is marked by the fluidity of the language and the 'realistic tone' of the narrative voice. The narration feels continuous even though it is extensively fragmented".[23] We could even say, therefore, that each entrance to a different narration, if existing, may always be "shrouded" and undistinguishable from the surroundings.

With this in mind, we return to the line cited above; now we have the impression that it is appropriate that such a line adorns the invisible entrance to the narration disguised as an imagined review. We must first note that this line contains, besides an entrance, such frequent motifs and ideas in this novel as "avenues," "to return" and "park" (also "night" is an important element which always casts a spell on otherwise drab streets in Berlin to transform them into magic, beautiful settings), and that this is the place where the word "entrance" appears for the first time in this novel. The line, moreover, cannot help attracting the reader with its mysterious imagery of the avenue that "had returned" for the night: the avenue is not there anymore (for it returned, perhaps to her home), thus making access to the park impossible, and the entrance to the park is covered with the coming darkness. The park, insulated and its entrance in mist, seems to exist as a kind of otherworld—a totally different space from the one in daytime. Now let us take a step backward from this line: we are now on the lines which sound very much like the true opening of Fyodor's review: "The collection opened with the poem 'The Lost Ball,' and one felt it was beginning to rain." Blackwell also sees the necessity for a short stop and an examination here: "What has happened in the space of the comma after 'Ball' ...? Evidently, a new voice, one of personal reminiscence, bursts into the tale. The language and imagery conform to a poet's, so we may presume that the lyrical narration is Fyodor's ...."[24] After this Blackwell proposes various narrative perspectives seen here using such terms as "Fyodor

[23] Blackwell, *Zina's Paradox*, 59.

– 128 –

Chapter IV Following Fyodor's Footsteps

the reviewer, Fyodor the reminiscer," etc. Anyway, he and most readers conclude that the part after the word "Ball" describes not the present Berlin but the past Petersburg evening. There is of course justice in this view, but it is also true that some reader cannot easily conclude thus, for the line in problem sounds so unnatural: we feel violently thrown into an unexpected place and time only by this small, common conjunction "and," and we wonder who the "one" who felt the rain is. So let us assume another possibility: the narrator here in this line refers to the present Berlin, in other words, the narrator is explaining he felt it was beginning to rain on the Berlin street just now (so the narrator is Fyodor the reviewer himself). If so, the reader is required to continue to read for a while by imagining two possible settings in parallel: the past Petersburg evening in the rain and the present Berlin one in the rain. It seems more reasonable, of course, to conclude it started raining in the past (in memory), as most readers do, but what seems more important here is the fact that the reader, perplexed and deferring his/her conclusion, forms the image of, to use the vocabulary of the novel, "twin" evenings: the overlapping cities of present Berlin and past Petersburg—the image underlying throughout the novel. One can safely say that the latter half of the line in problem reflects the present situation, for now it is evening, the sky is cloudy, and the city of Berlin in this novel has thousands of parks and avenues. To support this view, let us examine the following line that appears immediately after the auto-critique of Fyodor's poems seems to end: "When Fyodor went outside he felt immersed in a damp chill (it's a good thing I put that on): while he had been musing over his poems, rain had lacquered the street from end to end" (29; 215). The line happily proves it was really raining in the present Berlin. The rain started, possibly, when the protagonist threw himself on the couch and started to read his poems, so we may say the remark "one felt it was beginning to rain" does not necessarily refer to the

---

[24] Blackwell, *Zina's Paradox*, 64.

– 129 –

Reading Nabokov's Framed Landscape

past scene only. It is also noteworthy that the seemingly casual expression "from end to end" really makes us imagine that each end of the street cleverly fits with the opening and the ending of *Poems* (or of its review) respectively.[25]

The first entrance, therefore, belongs both to the past and to the present, leading the characters and the reader to a multifold world. *The Gift* consists of a series of entering and exiting from endlessly different and new worlds through various entrances and exits, visible or invisible. As the first entrance is shrouded, entrances in this novel tend to be uncertain: the door of Fyodor's new abode, for example, is "disguised by darkness" (53; 239), blocking the entrance of keyless Fyodor. Reading *The Gift* means to follow Fyodor's steps to keep pace with him, and to mark each elusive entrance, which proves to be more difficult than it seems.

As mentioned previously, the motif of covered entrance can be also a metaphor through which seamless, boundary-free shifts of narrative perspective can be explained.[26] The imagined review, most of which is read as Fyodor's childhood memory, for instance, does not have clearly distinguished opening (entrance) nor ending (exit), and the air of the present Berlin somewhat permeates this part of narrative. It must be noted that the medium which helps to merge the two worlds—the past Fatherland and the present Berlin—is the rain. Alexandrov notes "motifs linked to water imagery"[27] and suggests a "link between rain and life after death."[28] We may connect water imagery also with the theme of entrance: both the entrance and the exit of the narration under the guise of auto-critique are adorned with a reference to rain; we will also visit later another entrance

---

[25] This same street is revisited in Chapter 5 with a special emphasis on the idea of "ends."

[26] For the theme of boundaries see Blackwell.

[27] Alexandrov, *Otherworld*, 110.

[28] Ibid., 112.

– 130 –

Chapter IV Following Fyodor's Footsteps

which is surrounded with water imagery. Let us still linger for a while, however, on the entrance and the exit of this multi-layered world where a book of poems and the present, "real" Berlin merge.

The narrator informs us that *Poems* begins with "A Lost Ball" and ends with "The Found Ball." The way he introduces the last piece, however, is quite singular. After he examined a poem about watercolor (again "water") that seems the penultimate work in his collection, he sounds like terminating his review: "This, then, is Godunov-Cherdyntsev's little volume. In conclusion let us add ... What else? Imagination, do prompt me!" (28; 214). The narration then gradually shifts to the first person, making the reader guess that Fyodor's collection must end with the watercolor poem and that the review-like narration also came to a close. We soon notice the narrator and we are still in the review, and that the exit through which we felt getting out is a false one, as the narrator continues: "if a collection opens with a poem about 'A Lost Ball,' it must close with 'The Found Ball'" (28; 215), and the entire poem is shown. Is this poem really contained in *Poems*, or is it a spontaneous product imagined by the narrator? As this shows, the exit of both *Poems* and its pseudo-review are also shrouded.

What is also noteworthy is the absence of the word "ball" in the poem entitled "The Found Ball." The last three lines go as follows: "On the suddenly unmasked parquet, / Alive, and incredibly dear, / It was revealed in a corner" (29; 215). The idea that what was once lost returns governs the novel. Curiously, the tone and the rhythm of the lines above are almost identical with those of the part describing the return of Fyodor's dead father. In the last chapter, in Fyodor's dream, his explorer father, who is supposed dead comes back to see Fyodor, and the expression "his return, unharmed, whole, human, and real" (354; 530) echoes the poem. Moreover, the adjectives "alive" and "dear" which modify the ball (though the word "ball" itself does not exist in the poem) seem more apt for a human being: actually Fyodor's "dear" father comes home "alive" in his dream. So we can say that the poem "Found Ball" serves both as the exit of Fyodor's auto-re-

– 131 –

Reading Nabokov's Framed Landscape

view and as a covered entrance to another, remote scene—father's return.

Before we head to the next narrative fragment, let us examine still another entrance found in Fyodor's review. The entrance in the following extract to the park may be the same one that appeared at the opening of the review: "At the entrance to the public park we have the balloon vendor; above his head, three times his size, an enormous rustling cluster" (19; 206). Little Fyodor gets the biggest balloon from the vendor—the white one "with the rooster painted on it and the red embryo floating inside, which, when its mother is destroyed, will escape up to the ceiling and a day later will come down, all wrinkled and quite tame" (19; 206). Incidentally, the red embryo, though given birth and freed from its mother, finally reaches to the ceiling, that is, the boundary, which makes a contrast to what will happen to Fyodor and Zina Mertz: they will be completely free from her mother and from their apartment too.

What should be remembered is the balloon vendor's flight here. He pushes off with his heels and "slowly begins to rise in an upright position, higher and higher into the blue sky" (19; 206). He was standing at the entrance to the park, but he does not enter there nor walks away: he flies into the air towards an unknown destination. His unexpected move, therefore, suggests that this entrance is not only for the horizontal world but for vertical space which extends towards the sky.

In *The Gift*, the verb "enter," related to the entrance theme, is used with considerable frequency, always with a special emphasis. For example, Fyodor's mother has the belief that her husband is "convalescing after some long, long illness—and suddenly, flinging open the door noisily, stamping on the step, he would enter" (87; 270). We have the impression that by the words "the door" and "the step" in this context the narrator does not mean those of a specific room (house): they could equally refer to the entrance of the Petersburg home, of her apartment in Paris, or of Fyodor's Berlin apartment, and so possibly are just being used as just an image. As this line ends with the verb "enter" only, not reading "enter the room" or so, his

Chapter IV Following Fyodor's Footsteps

act of entering itself seems to be focalized especially. He does not just come back home alive; for some reason his return is characterized by these three steps of action with a noise: to fling open the door, to stamp on the step, and to enter. Most important is that this image is repeated in his return realized in Fyodor's dream (354; 530).

Another important example of "entering" imagery is in the following phrase: "Pushkin entered his blood" (98; 280). Fyodor closely studies Pushkin's works in order to compose his own father's biography. As a result, the boundaries between the world of Pushkin's fiction and Fyodor's "reality" dissolves, allowing characters of Pushkin to enter into Fyodor's world: "Towards him out of a Pushkin tale came Carolina Schmidt.... Beyond Grunewald forest a post master who resembled Simeon Vyrin (from another tale) was lighting his pipe by the window" (97; 280).

To enter, therefore, the central action of this novel, also implies the image of dissolving boundaries. The narrator continues to create this image by founding many entrances and exits—some of these almost invisible and in unexpected places. The narrator's verbal translation from several pictures is, as we have already discussed, one example: it helps to bore a loophole between the painting and the world of the story ("real" world), allowing characters and other materials to enter the other side (such as the "real" canary escaping into a painting).

Among the many entrances in *The Gift*, the following is perhaps the most problematic, closely connected with the complicating shifts of narrative perspectives. It appears towards the end of the novel, where Fyodor visits the Grunewald forest:

> At the end of the boulevard the green edge of the pinewood came into sight, with the gaudy portico of a recently constructed pavilion ..., through which—according to the scheme of the local Lenôtres—one had to go in order to enter at first a newly laid-out rock garden, with Alpine flora along geometric paths, which served—still according to that same scheme—as a pleasant threshold to the forest.

－133－

But Fyodor turned to the left, avoiding the threshold: it was nearer that way. The still wild edge of the pinewood stretched endlessly along an avenue for automobiles, but the next step on the part of the city fathers was inevitable: fence the whole of this free access with endless railings, so that the portico became the entrance of *necessity* (in the most literal, elementary sense). I built this ornamental thing for you but you weren't attracted .... (330; 504-5)

The narrative here is not easy to understand because of the narrator's densely textured style. So we are compelled to be "attracted" to the entrance by the way it is described. Now that we know the importance of the ideas of "threshold" and "entrance," we cannot just pass by the expression "the entrance of *necessity*." Moreover, the narrator devotes a considerable space to describe this entrance, which alludes to its singularity. What strikes us as most confusing is the last phrase above. The "I" who "built" this should be the narrator and the "you" means firstly Fyodor the protagonist and secondly, perhaps, the reader, for we are now trying to keep pace with him. We keep walking with Fyodor, looking sideway but somewhat closely at the "ornamental thing." Now it seems reasonable to suppose that this "ornamental thing" signifies not only the actual portico itself but also the whole of the long, detailed (thus looking ornamental as a result) description of the entrance cited above. In other words, what we encounter is on one hand the actual entrance (threshold) to the forest and on the other the process of decoratively telling about the entrance which itself leads to constructing a kind of entrance to some new dimension: we sense that after the passage above the narrator gradually comes to assume a different voice by entering another's (maybe Fyodor the character's) body.

We (the reader, Fyodor as the hero, and the narrator) step into the next paragraph (corresponding to the forest) not using the authorial entrance but a short-cut; this short-cut is cleverly and invisibly set in the long passage above. For our convenience, let us temporarily call the passage quoted above "entrance passage" (several more lines follow this passage to com-

Chapter IV Following Fyodor's Footsteps

plete the present paragraph, but here I have cut them) and the paragraph that follows "forest paragraph." We come to notice that in the forest paragraph that begins with the sentence "The forest as I found it was still alive, rich, full of birds" (330; 505), the "I" gradually morphs into a different existence. In the entrance passage, the "I" who built the entrance is the narrator. So when we find in the next paragraph such phrase as "The forest as I found," we naturally, continuously, regard the "I" as the same voice with this narrator. However, the last line of this forest paragraph proves the subtle shift of the narrative perspectives:

But careful: I like to recall what my father wrote: "When closely— no matter how closely—observing events in nature we must, in the very process of observation, beware of letting our reason—that garrulous dragoman who always runs ahead—prompt us with explanations which then begin imperceptibly to influence the very course of observation and distort it ...." (330; 505)

As he says "my father" and cites the words of the explorer father, we conclude that the voice is not the narrator's but Fyodor the character's. We could imagine that the "I" in the entrance passage imperceptibly enters Fyodor the character's body in the process of crossing to the forest paragraph.

The explanation above, however, is not precise, for the transition of different levels of first-person narration here is really more convoluted, permitting more than one interpretation. For example, the forest paragraph seems to be characterized with the theme of mimicry, as the narrator shows "a redheaded woodpecker" that is "imitating its own rap vocally" and a grasshopper imitating the stripes of the fallen pine needles or even their shadows (330; 506). It is no exaggeration to say that the idea of deception or mimicry is also reflected in the narrator's voice itself: it sounds as if the narrator, using first person narration, was imitating Fyodor the character's voice.

It is still fair to say that the passage quoted first forms the entrance to the next paragraph—a completely different space, which is, at the same

– 135 –

time, the forest and a new phase of narration. Also we should not ignore the fact that Fyodor enters the forest not by, in a word, the authorial entrance but by an unknown (at least to the reader) short-cut. Curiously, the same pattern appears in Fyodor's dream where his father returns: "He found his street, but at the end of it a post with a gauntleted hand on it indicated that one had to enter from the other end where the post office was .... But he was afraid of losing it in the course of a detour ..." (353; 529). These are the examples of Fyodor's disobedience, but suggest a paradoxical, elusive feature of entrances in this novel as well: entrances do exist, but in many cases uncertain, "shrouded" or "disguised," looking very near but actually very far, as if refusing a person's entrance. Despite this, paradoxically, we are steadily led to a succession of entrances to many different dimensions with their own unique style of narration.

Following Traces

Fyodor incessantly steps into many different dimensions—the past homeland, Central Asia, dream Berlin and so on—through vague entrances, sometimes even avoiding an authorized, formal one. A significant idea dominating such transfers of the protagonist is "walking." If we dare to call Nabokov's English masterpiece *Lolita* a road novel, we could call *The Gift* a pedestrian novel. The protagonist keeps walking through the streets of Berlin, into Grunewald, into the imagined mountain paths of Asia. There are good reasons for thinking such a seemingly commonplace act of walking should really be given a kind of privilege in this novel. *The Gift* abounds with the word "step," with remarks on shoes, with descriptions of streets, and with episodes related to promenades.

As Alexandrov explains the footprint motif with its connection to otherworld, this is obviously one of the most important motifs in the novel.[29] We will demonstrate how the novel is composed of the repeated act of imprinting the footsteps and following them, by expanding the footprint mo-

− 136 −

Chapter IV Following Fyodor's Footsteps

tif into the motif of "trace."[30]

First let us examine the act of "walking." In this novel it often happens that a walk is accompanied by conversation, which in turn is closely linked to Fyodor's creative, artistic activity. There are several occasions when Fyodor is forced to walk home because of lacking enough money for the tramcar. However, he always proves to have luck in finding a priceless gift from his money-free walking: walk on the street—mostly evening or night one—seems to work magic on Fyodor's imagination and his artistic mind.

The first evening of the novel is already connected to a verse composition. On the way to the Chernyshevskis' where they hold a literary party, his footsteps coincide with the ringing sound of a yet unborn poem in his mind, so he is in a sense "not quite knowing whether he is in the middle of the street or in the middle of the sentence."[31] After the literary soirée at the Chernyshevskis', Fyodor realizes he forgot to borrow money from Alexander Yakovlevich (Chernyshevski), so he, "who did not have money for the streetcar, was walking home" (52; 238). After this, several similar remarks emphasizing the act of walking are repeated, such as "He was walking along streets that had already long since insinuated themselves into his acquaintance" or "he walked along these dark, glossy streets" (53; 238). Here again he walks with the feeling that "there was some line of thought he had not pursued to its conclusion that day" (53; 238), that is, he is still in the state of walking with the murmur of an inchoate piece of poetry.

---

[29] Alexandrov, *Otherworld*, 111.

[30] In Nabokov's works "traces" (or "marks") are almost always a special device. In *Lolita*, for instance, Humbert Humbert, before first meeting Lolita, comes upon Lolita's marks such as an old tennis ball, the core of an apple, a white sock, etc.; the journey of Lolita and Humbert leaves "a sinuous trail of slime" (176). For a further analysis of Lolita's traces, see Wakashima, 『ロリータ、ロリータ、ロリータ』. In *The Gift*, the theme of following traces seems especially significant.

[31] Thus Nabokov describes Akaky Akakyevich, Gogol's protagonist in *The Overcoat* (*Nikolai Gogol* 146).

– 137 –

He finally reaches his apartment, but as mentioned before, he has no key; his entrance refused, he is perplexed and again "began pacing the sidewalk to the corner and back" (54; 239). The narrator then shows how this "echoic and completely empty" sidewalk seems to whisper into his ear the right words for a new poem. This image is clearly suggested in the following passage:

> He was somnambulistically talking to himself as he paced a nonexistent sidewalk; his feet were guided by local consciousness, while the principal Fyodor Konstantinovich, and in fact the only Fyodor Konstantinovich that mattered, was already peering into the next shadowy strophe, which was swinging some yards away and which was destined to resolve itself in a yet-unknown but specifically promised harmony. (55; 240)

As the excitement in this passage shows, Fyodor, once refused the entrance, continues to walk, talking to himself, and luckily enters into a world full of artistic stimulation and ringing, attractive phrases.

The scene of the first night of the novel thus shapes a basic pattern which will evolve in many ways throughout the book: the pattern where walking and dialogue are intertwined. Later, Fyodor's ambulatory dialogue with himself occurs in another form, as the imagined promenade with his fellow poet Koncheyev. This dialogue on foot begins with a highly impressive sentence: "Stupishin went to wait for a rare, almost legendary streetcar, while Godunov-Cherdyntsev and Koncheyev set out in the opposite direction, to walk as far as the corner" (70; 255). First of all, the "legendary streetcar" this Stupishin is supposed to take attracts our curiosity. This enigmatic man is said to move in and out so frequently (the same is true with Fyodor himself) and so far from the center of Berlin that "these changes ... seemed to others to happen in an ethereal world, beyond the horizon of human worries" (70; 255). The narrator does not make any further mention of this man, so he remains really a legendary character living "beyond the horizon" of the book. Moreover, his rare streetcar and the

$-138-$

Chapter IV Following Fyodor's Footsteps

beautiful way he proceeds imply the infinite space and possibility of this Berlin specially created by Nabokov.

In contrast, Fyodor and Koncheyev "set out in the opposite direction, to walk as far as the corner"—their way is described quite simply. At the corner, however, where they are expected to part, Fyodor calls Koncheyev to stop, saying "I don't have to expound to you on the black enchantment of stone promenades" (71; 255). They thus continue to walk together, talking mainly about Russian Literature. This, however, proves to be a fictitious walk and conversation imagined by Fyodor. In the promenade quoted previously, he walks down to the corner of his street and then goes back, entering a poetical dimension where he talks with himself; in the latter case, similarly, at the corner of the street, he steps into another narrative dimension and starts a conversation with an imagined Koncheyev. This imagined dialogue is far from fruitless.

Another impressive promenade occurs after the funeral of Alexander Yakovlevich Chernyshevski. Nabokov characters sometimes take a walk immediately after the death of a person very close to them, noticing the unusual appearance of their surrounding world. Fyodor, like these others, sets out on a walk after his friend's funeral:

> Upon the conclusion of the service the mourners, according to the scheme of the crematorium's master of ceremonies, were supposed to go up to the widow and one at a time and offer words of condolence, but Fyodor resolved to avoid this and went out onto the street. (313; 487-8)

One may notice the familiar expression "according to the scheme of" and Fyodor's ignoring this very scheme: an identical situation could be found at the entrance to Grunewald as has already been discussed (let me quote again: "through which—according to the scheme of the local Lenôtres— one had to go in order to enter ..."). That is to say, just like he avoids the authorized entrance at the forest, Fyodor refuses to obey the scheme to choose his own path.

– 139 –

Reading Nabokov's Framed Landscape

This time, perhaps, his ideal interlocutor should be the dead Cherny-shevski, but he cannot hear his voice nor does he even try to imagine con-versation with the dead man any more. He tries "to confess something" (314; 488) to Chernyshevski, but he cannot focus on the death nor catch his voice. This elusive walk in which he tries to catch what he longs to hear resembles to that poetic walk on the first evening of the novel. The narrator continues to describe every detail of the streets which Fyodor sees during his long walk. Fyodor, walking the streets, "tried to think about death" and "tried to imagine some kind of extension of Alexander Yakov-levich beyond the corner of life" (314; 488). However, he is distracted, cannot focus on the idea of death, and his attention is attracted only to the details of the streets with their parks and the expression of the sky. From this walk, however, he somehow notices with relief the existence of some-one who is responsible to everything and weaves "a magnificent fabric" (314; 488) of life. This promenade, therefore, again gives him a subtle gift.

As for a walk in quest of the marks of the dead, we must not ignore Fyo-dor's imagined walk with his father. As we saw in Chapter 1 of this thesis, he joins his father's caravan through the entrance disguised as the picture of Marco Polo. He follows his father's footsteps and gradually his feet become indistinguishable from his father's: he literally puts himself in his father's shoes, speaks with his father's voice as the first person narration voices gradually shift. The most memorable passage which shows how Fyo-dor really steps on the mountain paths is the following: "the flowers were filmed with rime and had become so brittle that they snapped underfoot with a surprising, gentle tinkle" (121; 304-5). We can almost hear the tin-kling steps of father and son, and moreover, the English version, with its group of similar sounds like "brittle," "gentle" and "tinkle," intentional or not, seems to augment the excitement felt through Fyodor's feet.

Towards the end of this exploration there appear motifs of traces and marks (note that in the following sentence the "I" indicates not Fyodor but his father): "In this desert are preserved traces of an ancient road along

– 140 –

Chapter IV Following Fyodor's Footsteps

which Marco Polo passed six centuries before I did: its markers are piles of stones" (124; 308). As mentioned above, the footprints motif is a part of a wider, central theme of "traces." Here, the idea of following person's marks and traces can be observed as a dual structure: Fyodor is following the footsteps and marks of his Father, who is in turn following those left by Marco Polo. Here, therefore, footprints and traces of three persons mix together.

Fyodor's father, by following the marks left by Polo, creates his own paths and his world, while Fyodor is also encouraged by father's marks, as we will see now. By picking up and recording his father's traces, Fyodor attempts to recreate the world once seen by his father. The following quotation demonstrates the special significance of marks and imprints: "As if playing a game, as if wishing in passing to imprint his force on everything, he [Fyodor's father] would pick out here and there something from a field outside entomology and thus he left his mark upon almost all branches of natural science" (112; 296). Although Fyodor dreams of completing a biography of his father by following the traces and walking with him, it is never realized, partly because he could not enter into the dark path in father's thoughts that is beyond his imagination.

The next point to make here is that there are several occasions where the narrator magically reproduces the original form from its trace. Take the following scene for example, first from the entrance: Fyodor, "crossing the square and turning into a side street," walks toward the tram stop "through a small, at first glance, thicket of fir trees" gathered for sale on account of the approach of Christmas. They form between them "a kind of small avenue," through which he walks, but "soon the tiny avenue broadened out, the sun burst forth and he emerged onto a garden terrace where on the soft red sand one could make out the sigla of a summer day" (85; 265). It may be noticeable that the Russian original for "into a side street" goes "*na bokovuyu ulitzu.*" Nabokov sometimes imprints his own name in this way on his work, and here at least his sigla seems to signal his Russian

– 141 –

reader that we are now entering a new, singular dimension. As expected, Fyodor who was walking the winter Berlin streets now enters into the past, summer Russia. Let us examine the details of "the sigla of a summer day":

> ... the imprints of a dog's paws, the beaded tracks of a wagtail, the Dunlop stripe left by Tanya's bicycle, dividing into two waves at the turn, and a heel dent where with a light, mute movement containing perhaps a quarter of a pirouette she had slid off it to one side and started walking, keeping hold of the handlebars. (85; 268)

In spite of the fact that what Fyodor sees now (or imagines seeing) is just the traces on the sand, the readers feel as if they are really seeing the full figure of the dog and the bird and not their traces. More marvelous is the reproduction of Tanya's figure; it is so precise and ingenious that we can clearly see her every movement. So our impression after reading this passage is that we saw not the tracks of her bicycle but Tanya herself, substantial and whole, with her lively actions. Fyodor (the narrator) can reproduce her with her movement in detail only from the Dunlop traces and her footprints, and the reader then catches the whole (though described by only words) as an animated vision. We enjoy in this way the original form created from its traces.

As this example shows, in *The Gift*, the figure which is recovered by Fyodor the narrator's pen from its imprints sometimes looks so substantial and detailed that it can match the real object before one's eyes. This reminds us of a description concerning the "transparent shadow on the wall" of a bicycle that is "even more perfect in shape" than the bicycle itself (174; 354). Here, the shadow is endowed with a perfect shape, by the creative power of, possibly, the sun. So we could safely suppose that our narrator, imitating the sun producing a more perfect image than the original, could recapture clearer images of things that were really present but are now vanished.

In this novel the trace (also shadow) precedes the object, waiting to be given proper shape by the narrator. The same observation seems to apply

Chapter IV Following Fyodor's Footsteps

to the generation of the main characters of this novel. Though critics already pointed that Zina Mertz, the heroine of the novel, seems to be generated from Fyodor's poem, this may be true of Fyodor the protagonist himself.[32] During the first few pages of the book the hero remains somewhat elusive, the naming also postponed. The reader is informed of his name for the first time through the phrase "the hitherto unknown author Fyodor Godunov-Cherdyntsev" (8; 196) which is mischievously uttered by Alexander Chernyshevski through the telephone: what should be noted is the fact that this is a quotation from an invented review of Fyodor's verse collection. His name is thus introduced vaguely from a non-existent source.

Moreover, it is in Fyodor's pseudo-review (again a "review") where he is formally introduced to us: "From the accumulating poetical pieces in the book we gradually obtain the image of an extremely receptive boy . . . . Our poet was born on July 12, 1900, in the Leshino manor . . ." (12; 200). This extract gives us the impression that the presence of the poems antecedes the poet: to put it the other way round, the author of the poem emerges from the poem which is in turn a mark left by a poet. If we expand the argument, we may even say that *The Gift* itself is made from the traces, the "dust," of Fyodor's life, as he confesses to Zina that he will write "a remarkable novel" from "dust" that will remain after he shuffles, twists, or mixes everything (364; 539). What Fyodor does in this book is therefore walking the streets, noticing imprints to reshape the already (or still?) invisible objects.

The last trace we would like to focus on here is closely connected with yet another theme of "flight." Let us go back to Grunewald where Fyodor finds himself in "the exact spot where a small airplane fell on the other day: someone who was taking his girl for a morning ride in the blue got

---

[32] Boyd observes that Zina "steps at last as if from the poem and into the novel." See Brian Boyd, *Russian Years*, 467.

– 143 –

Reading Nabokov's Framed Landscape

overexuberant, lost control of his joystick, and plunged with a screech and a crackle straight into the pines" (331; 506). Fyodor continues, "I, unfortunately, came too late ... but one could still see the imprint of a daring death beneath the pines." A few days later "all traces had disappeared," the only mark of the young couple's death being "the yellow wound on the pine tree," thus leaving them completely forgotten. However, thanks to Fyodor, who does not overlook their trace and manages to retrieve their images, allowing them to replay their flight, their presence is strongly impressed on the reader's mind, surviving longer.

Some readers, furthermore, may be inclined to identify the couple with that which appeared only once, in passing, in Chapter 2. At the platform where Fyodor and his mother are waiting for her train for Paris, the narrator makes us notice a couple: "a pale, red-lipped beauty in a black silk coat with a high fur collar, and a famous stunt flyer; everyone was staring at him, at his muffler, at his back, as if expecting to find wings on it" (96; 279). This transient couple, leaving no trace, seems to be doomed to oblivion, but at the same time the resonant description makes oblivion unlikely for them.[33] We have no definite evidence that these two couples are identical, but at the same time we cannot reject this possibility: the flyer and his lover may be doomed to death in Grunewald. In the mind of a reader who does not recognize the dead couple, the first couple at the platform will neither die nor, paradoxically, survive as a memory; while for a reader who does not know whether to identify one couple with the other or not to, the first couple may die, but in compensation will subsist as an eternally unset-

---

[33] The stunt flyer's figure reminds us of a depiction of Demon in Nabokov's *Ada*, whose "long, black, blue-ocellated wings trailed and quivered in the ocean breeze ... (people turned to look)"(*Ada* 180). This is an allusion to Lermontov's verse "Demon." The demon lover in this poem has a tendency to kill his women, so one may suggest the possibility that the flyer here, inheriting this tendency, will kill his girl by acrobatics, just like the couple over Grunewald. Incidentally, at the time of the story, supposedly around 1926, stunt flying was already enjoying great popularity.

– 144 –

Chapter IV Following Fyodor's Footsteps

tled problem.

In his works Nabokov likes to picture flight (and acrobatics) with a mixed feeling of fear and admiration.[34] The theme of flight, therefore, sometimes implies Nabokov's favorite idea of conquering gravity, and the remarks on the flight in *The Gift* are no exception. In this novel where walking and stepping the earth are dominant images, a few rare moments of flight create a light, joyous atmosphere, though they are mostly connected to death—death, therefore, which seems not very tragic but, I dare say, on the contrary, even cheerful.

The impressive scene of flight, which echoes those of the couples above, appears as follows: "One happy and cloudless day in July, a very successful ant flight was staged: the females would take to the air, and the sparrows, also taking to the air, would devour them" (60; 245). In spite of the fact that the winged ants are devoured by the sparrows, it is still "successful" flight on a "happy" day: it reminds us of a circus acrobat which is free from the heaviness and darkness of death (though it is true that a circus has a slight smell of death).

The ants which are suddenly endowed with "prop-room wings" (60; 245) may recall the stunt flyer at the platform and the pilot who dies "a daring death" in the forest. Furthermore, ants, as Fyodor's fellow pedestrians, play subordinate parts quite effectively throughout the novel. This scene is very memorable because this is a moment when a being that is in daily life doomed to step with its feet on the earth abruptly soars to the air, entering an unusual dimension of life. The narrator uses the expression that the sparrows "devoured" them: they are not "killed" tragically but merely disappear from our sight as if by a conjuring, and perhaps they are transported to another dimension.

Fyodor's daily, habitual walk always makes him enter unexpectedly into

---

[34] For an example of curious airplane accident and stunt flying, see *Pale Fire* (note to line 71).

– 145 –

another, unusual space and time: if seen from another angle, it must look like an accident or a magic trick in which a man who has been there in front of our eyes until just now abruptly vanishes to some unknown space. The following line invites us strongly to this view: "He jumped a puddle ... and printed his sole on the edge of the road: a highly significant footprint, ever looking upward and ever seeing him who has vanished" (78; 261-2). His sudden step to another world here reminds us of these ants that are pedestrians in everyday life but for some reason gain wings and then disappear into the body of sparrows.

Toward the end of the book we meet a memorable scene: "Suddenly, in the frank evening sky, very high ... 'Look,' he said. 'What a beauty!' A brooch with three rubies was gliding over the dark velvet—so high that not even the hum of the engine was audible" (362; 537). Though the narrator is surely referring to an airplane, he makes no mention of the word "airplane" itself, instead insisting on it being a brooch, and so the word "plane" seems as if it has been swallowed up together with its drone in the deep sky. This image implies the possibility of another world beyond the sky where resides a Supreme Being (the author or Fate, for instance). Also it heralds the space "beyond the skyline of the page" (366; 541).

In addition, we must focus on Fyodor's question which follows the passage above: "She [Zina] smiled, parting her lips and looking upwards. 'Tonight?' he asked, also looking upwards." To whom is he asking? What does he mean to say after the word "Tonight"? After this he understands Fate's attempts to bring Fyodor and Zina together. With this in mind, we can deduce that he is asking this question to Fate (or the author) who should be beyond the sky, ruling his life. "Tonight" is the last night of the novel, but as the narrator insists it does not really finish, leaving the impression that Zina and Fyodor will, in the middle of the street, abruptly vanish and successfully step into another dimension. On the last page, in the sentence beginning with "When I walk with you like this," the "I" and the "you" become gradually one entity in which the narrator, Fyodor and

Chapter IV Following Fyodor's Footsteps

Zina all mix. The narrator continues: "we crawl, dawdle, dwindle in a mist—now we are almost all melted" (366; 541). They seem to become unable to walk, the asphalt disappearing, the boundaries of three persons effaced. It seems they all glide into an uncommon world from this everyday life, through the common act of walking. The scene of a silently gliding airplane, therefore, seems to predict their transition and the world beyond the skyline of the last page.

When explaining Fyodor's tendency to "be solitary and poor," the narrator inserts the following sentence in which we could find possibly an all-explaining idea: "And, as if to spite common fate, it was pleasant to recall how once in the summer he had not gone to a party in a 'suburban Villa'. . . or how the previous autumn he had not found time to communicate with a divorce bureau which needed a translator . . ." (83-4; 267). I must first clarify the fact that though the narrator does not say so, Fyodor missed the occasions to meet Zina due to his avoiding those meeting with people and thus spiting a "common fate." The expression we should note is "common fate." The Russian original of the adjective "common," which signifies here "prosaic" or "everyday," reads "*hodyachii*"—this means of course "ordinary," but its primary meaning is "able to walk" (or "walking"). So the English equivalent for this adjective should be "pedestrian" that signifies both "common" and "related to walk." What is interesting is that Fyodor at first underrates Fate as a common, down-to-earth pedestrian, but at the end he appreciates her ingenuity: Fate is successfully elevated from Fyodor's fellow walker to a high status, beyond the reach of the characters. Fate herself, like other characters, ceases to walk and flies up to the air (at least in Fyodor's point of view, for Fate, from the very first, must really be lightly, imperceptibly soaring very high). *The Gift*, though named "a pedestrian novel," is always ready to award wings to all promenaders.

Let us go back to the place where we started our discussion to draw a good circle: "The avenue had returned from the park for the night, and its

– 147 –

Reading Nabokov's Framed Landscape

entrance was shrouded in dusk." Besides Fyodor and ants, everything in the novel, like this avenue, is able to walk and to disappear as by magic.[35] In the midst of their prosaic act of walking they suddenly seem to gain wings to enter a dimension different from common life. So the traces the reader tries to follow suddenly break off. As Nabokov in his English Foreword wonders "how far the imagination of the reader will follow the young lovers after they have been dismissed," it is not easy to follow their elusive footprints. They will find they do not have the key to their apartment, but we do not need to regard this negatively: they are finally free from the house which has always obstructed their love, so its door abandoned its role as the entrance, becoming the eternal exit.

When we visit that first park already familiar to us, this time in the Russian original, we find there, curiously enough, not the entrance but "vyhod," that is, "exit": in the English version the park is described as having an entrance, while the original an exit (again intentional or not).

When we walk along the lines in the English version of *The Gift* and lose our way, the exit—in the sense of solution—may be found in the original.

---

[35] As is often the case with Nabokov's work, trees are seen as good walkers: we encounter "a young chestnut tree" which is "still unable to walk alone" (59; 245); or pine trees which are described through the metaphor of marching (329; 503-4).

– 148 –

Conclusion

In *The Gift*, we can find the following passage immediately before the
one dealing with the shrouded entrance / exit of the park examined in our
last chapter:

> as he read, he again made use of all the materials already once gath-
> ered by his memory for the extraction of the present poems, and re-
> constructed everything, absolutely everything, as a returning traveler
> sees in an orphan's eyes not only the smile of its mother, whom he
> had known in his youth, but also an avenue ending in a burst of yel-
> low light and that auburn leaf on the bench, and everything, every-
> thing. (9-10; 197)

We have already had a glimpse of this line in Chapter III of this thesis,
where we examined the bench theme. As briefly mentioned, the original
of this "avenue ending in a burst of yellow light and that auburn leaf on the
bench" is quite possibly found in Nabokov's own memory: "the carved
back of a bench on the left, the alley of oaklings beginning beyond the
bushes honeysuckles" that the 5-year-old Nabokov drew on his pillow (the
Russian for "avenue" in the cited line from *The Gift* above reads " аллея,"
echoing the "alley" in the citation form *Speak, Memory* here). This avenue
(or alley) of oaks is granted a great importance in *Speak, Memory*, for this is
the place where he established "the inner knowledge that I was I and that
my parents were my parents":

> I became acutely aware that the twenty-seven-year-old being, in
> soft white and pink, holding my left hand, was my mother, and that
> the thirty-three-year-old being, in hard white and gold, holding my
> right hand, was my father. Between them, as they evenly pro-
> gressed, I strutted, and trotted, and strutted again, from sun fleck to
> sun fleck, along the middle of a path, which I easily identify today
> with an alley of ornamental oaklings in the park of our country es-

tate, Vyra . . . . (*SM* 19)

This recollection of "revelation" is associated with "strong sunlight" and "lobed sun flecks," (*SM* 18), which reminds us of the relation between the sun image and consciousness discussed in Chapter III. A reflection of this sunlight can be observed in the "burst of yellow light," which awaits Fyodor at the exit of the "avenue" in *The Gift*.

We thus safely arrive once again at the first scene discussed in the present dissertation: the promised "anastomosis" has occurred.

We started our discussion with the image of the 5-year-old Vladimir following the remembered alley leading to his country house with his forefinger, through which our author Nabokov could almost feel the earth of this beloved avenue. Through that invisible picture drawn on the white pillow we stepped into the world of Nabokov's landscape, as these little Nabokovs do in his own works; this exploration led us to the conclusion that his finger painting might be the original form of Nabokov's (and his character's) favorite, imaginative picture drawn with a white crayon pencil. The author Nabokov, by replacing the white crayon with a pencil, was able to draw as imaginative and colorful verbal pictures as those produced with the white, and made it possible to adopt the merits both of the visual art and of the verbal one: he can arrest time and allow a beloved image or scene to congeal by drawing it like a visual picture; he at the same time gives movement, sound and life to a work of visual art by translating it into language, dissolving the boundary between two arts and making his text richer and more profound.

The frames of those pictures invite the next motif—the window motif. The view from a window proved to be an essential component of Nabokov works; from these windows the attentive reader could get a glimpse of an unexpectedly multifaceted, profound landscape woven in Nabokov texts. From Fyodor's window, then, we attempted to share the Berlin view, with the hope of producing a map of Fyodor's Berlin. We, however, failed to do

Conclusion

so, because of the deceptive, mimetic nature of his recreated city, which seems to keep generating unidentified, temporary squares that are disconnected with each other. Fyodor finds a pleasure and importance in walking barefooted, therefore the touch of the earth felt through his bare foot is a dominant feeling throughout the novel: this way of generating topography in the world of his work by making a character feel the street with his own feet brings the reader back to the possible feeling the 5-year-old Vladimir might had when he tried to produce an invisible map, a plan, of his country estate with his finger. Keeping pace with Fyodor, and visiting one square / bench after another, we encountered unexpected, secret entrances, exits and paths impossible to be drawn on a map. In doing so, we were allowed to share a synesthetic moment with the author: sensing the paths through the feet in the process of recreating them with his finger or pen.

Fyodor's Berlin is too multidimensional, too imaginative, and too disjointed to be put down as a visible map on a sheet of paper. We could dare call it the transparent nature of the Berlin map of Fyodor's version, which naturally launches us back to our point of departure—the invisible but highly detailed, brilliant picture on the pillow. All the motifs by which we stopped during our partly peripatetic journey—white pencils, landscape, window views, city maps, squares, benches, entrance / exit and letters—thus proved to be subtly intertwined, finally joined together by the "blissful anastomosis," in the image of a child's finger following his beloved path and magically recreating other minute details. Nabokov's works look extremely visual, enticing the reader to translate those described images into pictures. Still, we will be aware of the fact that there remain the parts that cannot be depicted visually. Fyodor's Berlin, which seems at first view to be able to be precisely rendered as a map, turns out to be impossible to be completed as a proper map, every part being disconnected to each other. We can only see the city as if from numbers of small windows, as a cutout and framed landscape, and not as a bird's-eye view of the entire city.

– 151 –

However, this very fragmentary nature of the city allows the reader the pleasure of discovering those secret paths and entrances connecting each severed part. On this journey Nabokov readers are expected to visualize in their own mind the paths that the author secretly drew with his forefinger or a white pencil, and in the very pleasure of this discovery find themselves bestowed with a priceless gift from Nabokov.

WORKS CITED

AND CONSULTED

Alexandrov, Vladimir E. *Nabokov's Otherworld*. Princeton: Princeton UP, 1991.

---., ed. The *Garland Companion to Vladimir Nabokov*, New York: Garland Publishing, INC, 1995.

Appel, Alfred, Jr., and Charles Newman, eds. Nabokov: *Criticism, Reminiscences, Translations and Tributes*. Evanston: Northwestern UP, 1971.

Barabtarlo, Gennady. *Aerial View: Essays on Nabokov's Art and Metaphysics*. New York: P. Lang, 1993.

Beaujour, Elizabeth Klosty. *Alien Tongues: Bilingual Russian Writers of the "First" Emigration*. Ithaca: Cornell UP, 1989.

Becker, Andrew Sprague. *The Shield of Achilles and the Poetics of Ekphrasis*. Lanham: Rowan & Littlefield, 1995.

Berdjis, Nassim Winnie. *Imagery in Vladimir Nabokov's Last Russian Novel* (Дар), *Its English Translation* (The Gift), *and Other Prose Works of the 1930s*. Frankfurt: Peter Lang, 1995.

Blackwell, Stephen H. *Zina's Paradox: The Figured Reader in Nabokov's* The Gift. New York: Peter Lang, 2000.

Boyd, Brian. *Vladimir Nabokov. The Russian Years*. Princeton: Princeton UP, 1990.

---. *Vladimir Nabokov. The American Years*. Princeton: Princeton UP, 1991.

---. *Nabokov's* Pale Fire: *The Magic of Artistic Discovery*. Princeton: Princeton UP, 1999.

---. *Nabokov's* Ada: *The Place of Consciousness*. Ann Arbor: Ardis, 1985. Rev. edn. Christchurch, NZ: Cybereditions, 2001.

Boyd, Brian, and Robert Michael Pyle, eds. *Nabokov's Butterflies: Unpub-*

– 153 –

lished and Uncollected Writings. Boston: Beacon Press, 2000.

Connolly, Julian W. *Nabokov's Early Fiction: Patterns of Self and Other*. Cambridge: Cambridge UP, 1992.

---., ed. *Nabokov's* Invitation to a Beheading: *A Critical Companion*. Evanston: Northwestern UP, 1997.

---., ed. *Nabokov and His Fiction: New Perspectives*. Cambridge: Cambridge UP, 1999.

---., ed. *The Cambridge Companion to Nabokov*. Cambridge: Cambride UP, 2005.

Davidov, Sergei. "Weighing Nabokov's Gift on Pushkin's Scales." In *Cultural Mythologies*, 415-428.

De Botton, Alain. *The Art of Travel*. London: Penguin, 2003.

De Bries, Gerard, D. Barton Johnson with an essay by Liana Ashenden. *Vladimir Nabokov and the Art of Painting*. Amsterdam: Amsterdam UP, 2006.

Dolinin, Alexander A. "Foreword and Notes." *Vladimir Nabokov. Sobranie sochinenii russkogo perioda v 5 Tomakh*, T4. St. Peterburg: Symposium, 2000.

---. *"The Gift,"* in Alexandrov (eds.). *The Garland Companion to Vladimir Nabokov*, 135-68.

---. "Nabokov's Time Doubling: From *The Gift* to *Lolita*." *Nabokov Studies*, 2 , (1995), 3-40.

Elsner, Jaś. *Art and the Roman Viewer: The Transformation of Art from the Pagan World to Christianity*. New York: Cambridge UP, 1995.

Field, Andrew. *Nabokov: His Life in Art*. Boston: Little, Brown and Co., 1967.

Foster, John Burt, Jr. *Nabokov's Art of Memory and European Modernism*. Princeton: Princeton UP, 1993.

Gasparov, Boris, Robert P. Hughes, Irina Paperno. Ed. *Cultural Mythologies of Russain Modernism: From the Golden Age to the Silver Age*. *Berkeley*: U of California P, 1992.

WORKS CITED AND CONSULTED

Gibian, George, and Stephen Jan Parker, eds. *The Achievement of Vladimir Nabokov*. Ithaca: Center for International Studies, Cornell University, 1984.

Grayson, Jane. *Vladimir Nabokov*. Penguin Illustrated Lives. London: Penguin, 2001.

Heffernan, James A.W. *Museum of Words: The Poetics of Ekphrasis from Homer to Ashbery*. Chicago: U of Chicago P, 1993.

Homer. *The Iliad*. Trans. E.V. Rieu. 1950; rev, ed. London: Penguin, 2003.

Hyde, G. M. *Vladimir Nabokov: America's Russian Novelist*. Critical Appraisals Series. London: Marion Boyars, 1977.

Johnson, D. Barton. *Worlds in Regression: Some Novels of Vladimir Nabokov*. Ann Arbor: Ardis, 1985.

Karlinsky, Simon, ed. *Dear Bunny, Dear Volodya: The Nabokov-Wilson Letters, 1940-1971*. Revised and expanded edition. Ed., annotated, and with an introductory essay by Simon Karlinsky. Berkeley: U of California P, 2001.

Meyer, Priscilla. *Find What the Sailor Has Hidden: Vladimir Nabokov's* Pale Fire. Middletown: Wesleyan UP, 1988.

Nabokov, Vladimir. *Ada, or Ardor: A Family Chronicle*. 1969. New York: Vintage, 1990.

---. *The Annotated Lolita*, ed. with preface, introduction, and notes by Alfred Appel, Jr., 1970; rev, ed.: New York: Vintage, 1991.

---. *Bend Sinister*. 1947. New York: Vintage, 1990.

---. "Cloud, Castle, Lake." *The Stories of Vladimir Nabokov*. 430-437.

---. *Dar. Vladimir Nabokov. Sobranie sochinenii russkogo perioda v 5 Tomakh*, T4. St. Peterburg: Symposium, 2000, 191-541.

---. *The Defense*. Trans. Michael Scammell with the collaboration of the author. 1964. New York: Vintage, 1990.

---. *Despair*. 1966. London: Penguin, 2000.

---. *Drugie berega (s parallel'noi publikatsiei angliiskoi versii)*. Moscow:

-155-

Reading Nabokov's Framed Landscape

Zakharov, 2004.

---. *The Eye*. Trans. Dmitri Nabokov in collaboration with the author, 1965. New York: Vintage, 1990.

---. *The Gift*. Trans. Michael Scammell with the collaboration of the author. 1963. New York: Vintage, 1991.

---. *Glory*. Trans. Dmitri Nabokov in collaboration with the author. 1971. New York: Vintage, 1991.

---. "Hotel Room." *Poems and Problems*, 25.

---. *Invitation to a Beheading*. Trans. Dmitri Nabokov in collaboration with the author. 1959. New York: Vintage, 1989.

---. *Lectures on Literature*, ed. by Fredson Bowers. New York: Harcourt Brace Jovanovich/Bruccoli Clark, 1980,

---. *Lectures on Russian Literature*, ed. by Fredson Bowers. New York: Harcourt Brace Jovanovich/Bruccoli Clark, 1981.

---. "A Letter That Never Reached Russia." *The Stories of Vladimir Nabokov*, 137-140.

---. *Mary*. Trans. Michael Glenny in collaboration with the author. 1970. New York: Vintage, 1989.

---. *Nikolai Gogol*. New York: New Directions, 1961.

---. "Nomer v gostinitze." *Poems and Problems*. 24.

---. *Novels and Memoirs, 1941-1951*. New York: Library of America, 1996.

---. *Pale Fire*. 1962. New York: Vintage International, 1989.

---. *Pnin*. 1957. London: Penguin, 2000.

---. *Poems and Problems*. New York: McGraw-Hill, 1970.

---. *Priglashenie na Kazn'. Vladimir Nabokov. Sobranie sochinenii russkogo perioda v 5 Tomakh*, T.4. St. Petersburg: Symposium, 2000, 44-187.

---. *The Real Life of Sebastian Knight*. 1941. New York: Vintage, 1992.

---. "Recruiting." *The Stories of Vladimir Nabokov*, 401-405.

---. "The Return of Chorb." *The Stories of Vladimir Nabokov*, 147-154.

---. *Selected Letters, 1940- 1977*. Ed. Cmitri Nabokov and Matthew J.

WORKS CITED AND CONSULTED

Bruccoli. New York: Harcourt Brace Jovanovich / Bruccoli Clark Layman, 1989.

---. *Speak, Memory: An Autobiography Revisited*. 1967. London: Penguin. 1989.

---. "Spring in Fialta." *The Stories of Vladimir Nabokov*, 413-429.

---. *The Stories of Vladimir Nabokov*. 1995. New York: Vintage International, 1995.

---. *Strong Opinions*. 1973. New York: Vintage, 1990.

---. *Transparent Things*. 1972. New York: Vintage, 1989.

---. *The Man from the U.S.S.R. and Other Plays*. Introductions and translations by Dmitri Nabokov. New York: Harcourt Brace Jovanovich / Bruccoli Clark, 1984.

---. "Ultima Thule." *The Stories of Vladimir Nabokov*, 137-140.

---. "The Visit to the Museum." *The Stories of Vladimir Nabokov*, 277-287.

Naumann, Marina Turkevich. *Blue Evenings in Berlin: Nabokov's Short Stories of the 1920s*. New York: New York UP, 1978.

Píchová, Hana. *The Art of Memory in Exile: Vladimir Nabokov and Milan Kundera*. Carbondale: Southern Illinois UP, 2002.

Pifer, Ellen, ed. *Nabokov and the Novel*. Cambridge, MA: Harvard UP, 1980.

Proffer, Carl R., ed. *A Book of Things About Vladimir Nabokov*. Ann Arbor: Ardis, 1974.

Proust, Marcel. *À la rechérche du temps perdu, Du côté de chez Swann, édition présentée et annotée par Antoine Compagnon*. Paris: Gallimard, 1987-8.

Pushkin, *Aleksandr, Eugene Onegin. A novel in Verse by Aleksandr Pushkin*. Trans. with commentary by Vladimir Nabokov, 2 vols., Bollingen Series 72. Paperback edition. Princeton: Princeton UP, 1990.

Rowe, William Woodin. *Nabokov's Deceptive World*. New York: New York UP, 1971.

Salehar, Anna Maria. "Nabokov's *Gift*: An Apprenticeship in Creativity"

-157-

in *A Book of Things about Vladimir Nabokov*. Ed. Carl R. Proffer. Ardis: Ann Arbor, 1974, 70-83.

Scammell, Michael, Yuri Leving. "Translation is a Bastard Form": An Interview with Michael Scammell. *Nabokov Online Journal*, Vol. I, 2007.

Semochkin, Aleksandr., ed. *Ten' russkoi vetki: Nabokovskaya Vyra*. St. Petersburg: Liga Plyus, 2002.

Shawen, Edgar McD. "Motion and Stasis: Nabokov's 'Cloud, Castle, Lake'", *Studies in Short Fiction*, 27: 3 (1990: Summer), 379-383.

Shrayer, Maxim. *The World of Nabokov's Stories*. Austin: Univ. of Texas P., 1999.

Stegner, Page. *Escape into Aesthetics: The Art of Vladimir Nabokov*. New York: The Dial Press, 1966.

Tammi, Pekka. *Problems of Nabokov's Poetics: A Narratological Analysis*. Suomalaisen Tiedeakatemian Toimituksia Annales Academiae Scientiarum Fennicae B231. Helsinki: Suomalainen Tiedeakatemia, 1985.

---. *Russian Subtexts in Nabokov's Fiction: Four essays*. Tampere: Tampere UP, 1999.

Toker, Leona. *Nabokov: The Mystery of Literary Structures*. Ithaca: Cornell UP, 1989.

Wagner, Peter. Ed. *Icons—Text—Iconotexts: Essays on Ekphrasis and Intermediality*. Berlin: de Gruyter, 1666.

Wood, Michael. *The Magician's Doubt: Nabokov and the Risks of Fiction*. Princeton: Princeton UP, 1995.

Wyllie, Barbara. *Nabokov at the Movies: Films Perspectives in Fiction*. Jefferson, NC: McFarland, 2003.

Zimmer, Dieter E. *Nabokov's Berlin*. Berlin: Nicolai, 2001.

秋草俊一郎 「ナボコフが付けなかった注釈：ナボコフ訳注『エヴゲーニー・オネーギン』を貫く政治的姿勢について」Slavistika XXIII 東京大学大学院人文社会学科研究科, 2007 年, 59-80.

諫早勇一 「ナボコフのロシア語作品と分身テーマ」『言語文化』第

WORKS CITED AND CONSULTED

2 巻第 4 号，2000 年，533 – 46.

工藤庸子 「フロベール的イントネーション」と『ロリータ』．日本
　　ナボコフ協会 2007 年度大会報告集　特集「ナボコフと世界文
　　学」　日本ナボコフ協会 2007　*Nabokov and World Literature: Pro-*
　　ceedings of the 2007 General Meeting of the Nabokov Society of Japan,
　　31-44.

若島正　『ロリータ、ロリータ、ロリータ』作品社, 2007 年．

◎著者紹介◎

Maya Minao Medlock

メドロック皆尾麻弥
1977 年鳥取県生まれ。佛教大学英米学科准教授。京都大学大学院
博士課程満期退学。文学博士。主な著書、論文に、『見てごらん
道化師を！』（翻訳）（作品社、2016 年）、「ハンバートの目にも涙」
（研究社『書きなおすナボコフ、読みなおすナボコフ』2011 年）、
「『ロリータ』の車窓から」（研究社「英語青年」総号 1910 号、
2009 年）、"In Search of a Mailbox—Letters in *The Gift*"（*Nabokov
Online Journal,* 2007 年）、"Entrance and Exit in Nabokov's *The Gift*"
（*Humaniora Kiotensia On Centenary of Kyoto Humanities,* Kyoto University, 2006 年）、「ナボコフのベンチを訪ねて」（日本英文学会『英
文学研究』第 82 巻、2005 年）。

MEDLOCK Minao Maya is associate professor at Bukkyo University, Kyoto. Her publications include "In Search of a Mail-
box---Letters in *The Gift*" (*Nabokov Online Journal*, 2007), "Entrance
and Exit in Nabokov's *The Gift*" (*Humaniora Kiotensia On Centenary
of Kyoto Humanities*, Kyoto University, 2006), and a Japanese translation of Nabokov's novel *Look at the Harlequins!* (Sakuhinsha,
2016).

佛教大学研究叢書33

Reading Nabokov's Framed Landscape

2018（平成 30）年 2 月 28 日発行

定価：本体6,700 円（税別）

著　者　メドロック皆尾麻弥

発行者　佛教大学長　田中典彦

発行所　佛教大学

〒603-8301 京都市北区紫野北花ノ坊町96
電話 075-491-2141（代表）

制　作
発　売　株式会社　英宝社

〒101-0032 東京都千代田区岩本町2-7-7
電話 03-5833-5870（代表）

印刷・製本　モリモト印刷株式会社

© Bukkyo University. 2018　ISBN978-4-269-74039-6　C3098

『佛教大学研究叢書』の刊行にあたって

二十一世紀をむかえ、高等教育をめぐる課題は様々な様相を呈してきています。科学技術の急速な発展は、社会のグローバル化、情報化を著しく促進し、日本全体が知的基盤の確立に大きく動き出しています。そのような中、高等教育機関である大学に対し、「大学の使命」を明確に社会に発信していくことが求められています。

本学では、こうした状況や課題に対処すべく、本学の建学の理念を高揚し、学術研究の振興に資するため、顕著な業績をあげた本学有縁の研究者に対する助成事業として、平成十五年四月に「佛教大学学術振興資金」の制度を設けました。本『佛教大学研究叢書』の刊行は、「学術賞の贈呈」と並び、学術振興資金制度による事業の大きな柱となっています。

多年にわたる研究の成果は、研究者個人の功績であることは勿論ですが、同時に本学の貴重な知的財産としてこれを蓄積し活用していく必要があります。また、叢書として刊行することにより、研究成果を社会に発信し、二十一世紀の知的基盤社会を豊かに発展させることに貢献するとともに、大学の知を創出していく取り組みとなるよう、今後も継続してまいります。

佛教大学